A Boomer Babes Book Club Romance

Charming Chapter

LORI HAAS

Morewellson, Ltd.

ISBNs: (e-pub) 978-1-950452-63-7 (standard paperback) 978-1-950452-64-4

Contents

A Boomer Babes Book Club Romance

Charming Chapter

LORI HAAS

Morewellson, Ltd.

Chapter One

A New Chapter

Laura's heart raced. On the outside, she looked no different from any of the other travelers. Yet as she made her way toward the plane's entrance, butterflies surged inside.

If only John could have come with me.

She wouldn't cry. Not here. Not now. Life had thrown them a curveball. She took a deep, steadying breath.

It'll be okay. I can do this.

She concentrated on the person in front. Why were they headed to London? Had they ever traveled solo before? She adjusted her shoulder bag. The person in front moved and she shuffled behind him, making their way down the jetway.

A tall and willowy flight attendant greeted her at the entry door. "Hello, may I help you find your seat?"

Laura glanced at the boarding pass she held. "4 A."

"Perfect. If you turn to your left here, it is the third cubicle from the front. Have a pleasant trip."

"You too." Laura chuckled at her goof. The woman probably heard the faux pas quite a lot.

The attractive woman smiled. "Thanks. I hope so too. Curious, has anyone ever told you that you look like Catherine Deneuve?"

Laura bathed in the kind words, a warmth penetrating inside. "No, but I appreciate the compliment. Thank you." Laura moved through the doorway, she scanned the numbers for her seat.

Laura sought to retain a cool, 'I do this all the time' exterior but struggled to contain her delight with flying first class. Four A. After dropping her purse onto the seat, she thrust her small carrier bag into the cubby. She removed her new coat, as an attractive dark-haired male approached. "May I take your coat for you?"

"Yes, that would be nice. Thank you."

After he returned, he bent close, with Laura catching a faint hint of musk. A trace of a French accent made his words flow like honey. "Would you like a glass of champagne before we take off?"

On a normal day, drinking champagne in the morning would be out of character for her. Her newfound friends from book club had goaded her to be open to enjoying herself to the fullest. She planned to do just that. "Yes, please."

After he'd left, she settled into her seat. She opened the various cubbies, taking stock of all the wonderful items on offer for her travels. She exhaled. Contentment wrapped around her like a warm blanket. Why had she waited all her life to experience some pampering? Well, she knew. Life, and all it entailed. It had been full of time spent raising kids, working various jobs, managing the home, and so much more. It had been rare for her to take time for herself over the years. Much less on something so extravagant as a first-class trip to London to look up her ancestry.

A lump formed in her throat as her thoughts traveled to more recent events. As John approached retirement, they had planned to enjoy all the traveling they'd never gotten around to in their youth. Sudden, unbidden tears sprung to her eyes.

Five years. John had been gone, but the pain still lingered. A sight. Smell. The worst was remembering a private joke they'd shared. No one else held the same memories. How they could glance at one another and know what the other was thinking. Grief's bubble had encased her for so long. A smile played on her lips at the knowledge she'd grown content. Thankful to no longer be looking in on life. She had joined the world again. Still, her heart healed, yet bore the cracks of her pain. Quiet laughter across the aisle brought her back to the present. A young couple, probably on their honeymoon or traveling together for the first time. Warmth filled her as she recalled those days of love's first blush.

"Here you are, Mrs. Rollins." The steward had returned with her champagne, its shade a golden blond. She took the goblet from him and thanked him before he moved off to another traveler. The fizzy drink delivered the taste of cherries and a yeasty flavor not unlike brioche. She relaxed against the leather seat as she brushed a stray lock of silky hair back behind her ear.

His use of her married name pulled her back into her thoughts. She was no longer a missus but certainly not a miss either. What did you become as a widow? Of course, she could have checked Ms. in the box but that term didn't fit either. She pulled up her phone, searching for the term dowager. She did have property from her late husband but the term designated a dignified elderly woman.

Laura shut down the app and set her phone on the tray. Elderly. Who decides what's elderly? She didn't consider herself old. As soon as she'd hit fifty-five, the membership paraphernalia had started arriving in her mailbox. Laura sipped the champagne.

Overthinking again. Can't you for once think of something good? When things had started changing—oh yes, after meeting the book club ladies.

Her mind drifted back to the first meeting. Serendipity. Isn't that what it was called? Something happens that affects you in more ways than you imagined.

She recalled her trip to the local bookstore. Something had drawn her to go inside. Entering the store, the smell of old books greeted her. Piles of books on every surface supplied a homey feeling. Laura browsed the various tomes on display. There might be some books that would make for good birthday or Christmas gifts. Laura had been flipping through the pages of a book when Angela walked over to her.

Laura paused from reading. The woman's face glowed radiant with good health, and Laura instantly liked the woman. They'd introduced themselves as they continued chatting. So, it didn't seem strange at all for Angela to ask her to join her for coffee at the café next door. They'd chatted about the books they'd bought, and about their lives. Now thinking back on it, it had been more about hers. That's when Angela shared about starting the book club. How she envisioned a small group and wondered if Laura would like to join. They'd meet once a month, enjoy dinner together, and discuss that month's book.

Laura knew she needed to get out more, and she loved books. She met the ladies at a restaurant, and they named themselves the Boomer Babes Book Club. She'd never thought of herself as a babe, but why not? With age should come the freedom to do and be what you want. So what if it took her to her sixties to realize that?

Laura giggled, recalling their first meeting. Angela had picked a group of ladies around the same age but in various life stages. Some were single, others were divorced or widowed. Only one had noted being married. There were even some fireworks with two ladies.

If not for her picking the first month, she doubted she'd have continued with the group. She'd picked historical fiction for her month with the classic book, *Rebecca*. Her choice also led to research beyond the book. She delved into learning more about her roots in the United Kingdom. Using an ancestry tool, Laura traced her roots back to the fifteen-hundreds. It was fun to see the Lords and Ladies in her lineage.

Over dinner, the group encouraged her to visit the places she'd shared. Despite her sharing her responsibilities, they dismissed her reasons for not going.

The eldest, Claire, had spoken first. "Your grandchildren have a mother. And your mother sounds like she can take care of herself. You should go."

Shirley followed Claire's statement. "If you have so many miles, your travel portion is paid. So there doesn't seem to be any reason you shouldn't go."

"Exactly! Plus, I bet I could hook you up with a pet sit. So you wouldn't have to worry about staying in a stuffy hotel all the time you're there." Betsy shared earlier how she'd done pet-sitting there before. It had allowed her to travel to other places too.

Before she'd known it, Betsy had contacted a couple who were heading to Morocco for a few weeks and would need a sitter for their dog. Everything had fallen into place with minimal effort. There was that serendipity again. If Laura hadn't known better, it appeared as if Angela had selected each woman for a specific purpose in the book club.

One woman in particular who'd forced her out of her comfort zone. After they'd all encouraged her to be brave and travel solo, Sylvie chimed in. "With that many miles, you must fly first class!"

"I don't know. That seems…"

"Like what? That you don't deserve or you should save it? From the brief time I've known you, it sounds like you're more than due for some splurging. You deserve it." Sylvie crossed her arms, daring Laura to refute her.

The quiet-spoken Francis had chimed in. "Yes, I wish I could go back and be more *in the moment* with my life. It goes by so fast. Consider it a birthday treat to yourself if that makes you feel better."

So Laura booked the flight, giddy with the prospect of exploring her roots. Then her growing excitement had come crashing down when she told her daughter about her trip arrangements.

"Mom, what are you thinking? You're in your sixties, for heaven's sake. You can't go traipsing around the world by yourself. Plus, what about Danielle? She'll need picking up from school and then there's Luke's—"

"You'll have to make other arrangements."

On most days, Laura would have backed down, but her book club friends had told her to practice that very statement over and over in the mirror. Once she felt confident that she wouldn't back down, she told Caroline.

In a huff, Caroline grabbed her bag. Her parting words were, "You're only thinking of yourself."

Laura waved from the door as her fuming daughter strode to her car. "Yes. Yes, I am. And I think it's about time."

The captain coming onto the speaker brought her back to the present. The captain had noted they were waiting for some additional luggage before taking off. She glimpsed her almost empty champagne goblet.

After a deep, contented sigh, Laura reclined in her chair while raising the footrest. She took a moment to pull out some lotion, slathering it on her hands before patting it on her face. While planning her trip, she'd found the tip to keep your skin from drying out on longer flights. As she placed the tube back in her purse, the handsome young steward came to her seat, asking if she'd like a refill. She almost said no.

I shouldn't. Says who?

"Yes, that would be nice."

From now on Laura, you better say 'yes' instead of constant no's.

Plus, it might make her sleepy earlier so she could get some rest on the trip over. She'd pulled up a rom-com movie by the time he returned with a fresh glass of champagne. "Please let me know if you would like anything else, madame. We will be taking off in a minute. Enjoy your trip."

She returned his smile. "Thank you. I plan to."

After eating a wonderful meal, Laura watched her movie until her eyelids grew tired. The champagne, coupled with the carb-heavy meal had done the trick. She lowered her seat to its flat position before drifting off to sleep. Thankful for a good solid sleep for four hours, she woke to the aroma of coffee brewing.

Excitement at nearing her destination finished waking her up. Laura moved into a seated position, stretching her arms, and yawning away the cobwebs. An attendant appeared with coffee and she requested a light breakfast.

I'll never want to travel in economy again.

It wasn't long before they were pulling up to the gate. Sylvie advised Laura to take advantage of the first-class arrivals lounge showers before leaving the airport. At first, it seemed senseless, but Sylvie said it would help wake her up before heading out to London. Plus, if she didn't eat on the plane, she could grab some breakfast or some snacks for later. With that plan in mind, Laura had chosen an outfit for the plane made for comfort more than looking stylish.

Laura took the time for a shower, dressing in clean, unwrinkled clothing. When she returned home, she'd have to thank Sylvie for her advice as the shower had refreshed and energized her. As it was already late morning, she enjoyed some items from the lunch buffet. That would save her from having to purchase lunch out somewhere or be hungry when she arrived at her destination.

After enjoying her meal, Laura made her way out to the taxi area.

This is it. The adventure begins.

Chapter Two

Handsome Stranger

"Taxi, ma'am?"

"Yes, please." She pulled her new bag behind her, the wheels beating a rhythm on the pavement. While Laura had purchased a train ticket for her time in London, she decided on a taxicab to take her to the house. Along the way, Laura hoped to enjoy seeing the various architecture and the double-decker buses. However, unlike most freeways in the states, everything rushed past, leaving her disappointed.

Her frustration changed to glee when they got off the highway and turned onto Kensington High Street. Now in the city's midst, the views were of modern and historical melded together. She marveled at the architectural combinations. Peering out her window kept her occupied, as did seeing the occasional double-decker red bus.

She grinned when the view turned to trees. She knew from her previous searches online, that it meant they were nearing her destination. Laura scooted closer to the window, keeping her eyes peeled.

There it is. It's huge.

She turned around to see the Albert Memorial spires disappearing.

Laura spoke to the driver, "Will we be going past the Royal Albert Hall on the way?"

"Certainly, ma'am."

After making their way around the enormous historic building, the driver drove on toward Queen's Gate. Arriving at the townhouse, Laura's breath caught. Her love for architecture and history came alive as she took in the white plaster buildings, black door fronts, and black iron railings. She recalled learning about some railings that were at one time used as stretchers back in World War Two. She'd have to see if she could find some while she stayed in London.

Counting the windows, each townhome must make up six to seven floors along with the basement. If not for the modern vehicles driving by, the home facade would be a vivid historical reminder.

Laura paid her driver before stepping out onto the sidewalk. The air was crisp with a few leaves dancing on the streets accompanied by the smell of wood burning in a fireplace. Popping a mint in her mouth, she settled herself for their first meeting. Mounting the five steps up to the front door, she rang the bell. A lovely chiming sound came from inside.

A middle-aged, petite woman wearing cream slacks and a twin cashmere sweater set opened the front door.

"Hello. You must be Laura." Her posh English accent delighted Laura who smiled at hearing it. The woman waved Laura into the house.

"Yes, and you must be Lavinia." Laura took her bag and placed it in the entry foyer.

Lavinia welcomed Laura warmly with a firm handshake. After a few moments about her trip, Lavinia showed Laura to the room she'd be using.

"I'll give you some time to get settled. Then we'd like to take you out for dinner tonight if that suits you."

"Yes, that'd be nice."

"Splendid. Don't hesitate to call out if you require anything."

"Thank you."

"I'll leave you to it then." Lavinia left the room so Laura could unpack. The room decor had been tastefully done with a bowl of lavender buds in a cut crystal bowl. Laura leaned over it, inhaling the earthy, yet sweet aroma. The sunny cream and blue bedroom overlooked the back garden. Even though fall would arrive soon, flowers still spilled from pots and along the walled garden.

How wonderful. I'd love a walled garden with a nice bench for reading. I need to thank Betsy for telling me about pet sitting and giving me this introduction.

It would save Laura money on her trip, plus it was so nice to stay in a home. And what a home. She'd only seen these homes from another era in pictures or movies. After unpacking her clothing and hanging them in the armoire, Laura strode over to the bathroom with her toiletry bag. Fiddling for the wall switch, she searched in vain.

It has to be here somewhere.

She fumbled along the wall. Nothing. She remembered seeing shows where the doorknobs were higher on the doors, so maybe the switches were too. She reached up over her head and groped with her hand along the wall.

A deep voice startled her. "May I help you?"

"Ack!" Laura cried out in surprise.

"My utmost apologies. I didn't mean to frighten you. The door was open." It was Lavinia's husband.

"All good. If you don't mind helping me, I can't seem to find the light switch."

He reached over on the other side from where she'd been hunting and pulled a chain. "No switches in the bathroom."

Color rose to Laura's cheeks. Of course, she'd read that somewhere. Why hadn't she remembered? Instead, she'd ended up looking foolish.

"Thank you."

"You're welcome. Lavinia asked if you would like to accompany her to walk the dogs before we make our way to the White Swan for dinner?"

"Yes. I'll just put on my tennis shoes and be down in a moment."

He nodded and left her to go back downstairs.

Ugh. I hope he doesn't think of me as a dotty old lady who didn't have a clue about anything. Who am I kidding? I am a dotty old lady to most younger people.

At least that's what her daughter, Caroline, implied. Her heart raced. This was a bad idea. What was she thinking? Coming across the world to explore her roots. She should have stayed home and saved money. She should have stayed in her comfort zone. She clamped her lips tight, inhaling deeply.

Stop 'shoulding' on yourself.

Laura peered at herself in the mirror. "But you didn't. Because you're not a dotty old woman. And don't you forget it." The woman in the reflection winked back at her.

Lavinia waited downstairs when Laura arrived, having changed into better walking shoes. Two well-behaved dogs sat at her feet, but their expressions bore excitement at this new stranger. Lavinia's laugh was infectious. "As you can see, one mustn't miss their walks." She handed Laura the leads.

"Hello, you two." She scratched behind their ears. "Now, you must be Geoffrey." She scratched his neck as she attached the lead. "And you, my dear, must then be Sophia. The spaniel wagged her tail. "I can see we'll be good friends."

Once they were situated, they made their way down the steps to the street. Lavinia shared a bit about the neighborhood, and Laura asked about the homes.

"Ours was built in the 1860s and designed by Richardson. Are you interested in architecture?"

"Yes, I'd considered becoming an architect when younger, but then I got married, and well—"

"Ah yes, the forgotten dream."

Laura almost stopped in her tracks. Had that been what had happened? Dreams set aside never to be achieved or even recognized. She took a deep breath, wondering what other forgotten dreams she'd had.

"Ah, here we are." Lavinia took Gregory's leash from Laura, and they crossed over to the wildlife park. Lush with foliage and blooming with color, even in the fall, it was a calm oasis from the busy city streets.

"We'll do a short walk at night for them and often take a longer walk during the morning. If you would like a longer walk for an outing, you can take them to the park by Kensington."

"That would be nice." That evening, they enjoyed dinner out at the busy pub before Laura fell into bed exhausted with jet lag.

A fter waving goodbye to the couple the following morning, she settled into a routine with the dogs. She noted how they would wake up early, which suited her, and they would go out for a walk in the cool of the morning. Back at the house, they would head to their pallets next to the Aga in the kitchen, where they would nap.

This gave her a chance to head out to see some sights on her list. Lavinia had also shared some places Laura might like to explore while in London. There were so many places within walking distance she wondered if she'd end up using her senior train pass. However, for those she'd added to her list, her rail pass would come in handy.

She decided there were some age advantages. And she would focus on the advantages versus the disadvantages while on her travels. As the next day looked to be nice weather, Laura bundled up before heading out for a longer walk. She wandered the streets, enjoying the architecture before making her way over to the gardens on the Kensington Palace grounds. She strolled with the dogs along the Flower Walk. She relished the leaves crunching underfoot.

Her thoughts were elsewhere when a pull on the leash surprised her. The leash dropped, and Laura scrambled to grab it. Sophia bolted away.

Oh no. She must have seen a squirrel. Lavinia had said Sophie had a fascination with them. While she wrestled to control an excited Geoffrey, Sophia ran barking toward a tree. Laura sprinted toward the dog. Well, as much as her non-runner legs could sprint.

Just as she reached for Sophia's leash, the dog bolted toward two gentlemen, who were deep in conversation. Sophia jumped toward one man.

"Madam, your b—!"

Laura stopped in shock. Had he just called her what she thought? Her mouth dropped open in shock. Anger rose as she fought the urge to give the man a piece of her mind. It's not like Sophia's paws were muddy. His pants looked fine after she'd jumped on him. Her gaze went to his face.

Under his stylish brown fedora, his tawny hair brushed over his ears, curling alongside them. No doubt signaling a trip to the barber overdue. Along his cheeks, a mixture of brown with some gray led to shorter sideburns. His long, straight nose led to his mouth and full lips. Then she met his eyes. A combination of gray and green, they connected with hers. She fought to look away but couldn't. As if their gaze toward each other had been magnetic, neither having a choice in the matter.

Well, so what that he's handsome. I'd much rather have a nice, polite man than a rude one. What are you even saying? Keep focused!

She grabbed the dog's lead, muttering under her breath, "Rude."

The tall, attractive man stared at her as his shorter companion spoke in a muffled voice, "Americans."

She turned back toward him. "Well, you're impolite. So there!" Her eyes grew wide. Had she just said that aloud? The man Sophia had jumped on stopped walking. He stared at her with those intense gray eyes but said nothing. Though his upturned lips were hard not to notice. He touched his finger to his hat as they walked away.

Impolite? That's your big put-down? You're impolite. I bet they're quaking in their boots now.

She gathered the leashes, wrapping them firmly with both hands. Her rage subsided, she strode away toward a bushy hedge. As she came to a nearby tree, her body shook with indignation. She might have been called that name in her lifetime but never out loud or to her face. The dogs looked at her as if reading her mind.

"See, Geoffrey? You'd never act that way. Come on Sophia, I think we've had enough excitement for one day." As she walked, the smell of coffee brewing from a kiosk caught her attention. A cup of coffee right now would be heavenly. She'd put the dogs up in the warm kitchen and walk back over to grab coffee later. It might settle her nerves and remind her that most people were decent human beings.

As she headed back toward the house, she chided herself on the fact that she kept thinking about the man. Yes, it still made her blood boil. Had that been the reason she'd felt so warm or flushed when their eyes met? Yes, he was handsome. A mustache shadow topped his full lips, and his jaw was firm for an older man. His quick reflexes displayed his physical health. It was harder to remain upset with someone who had sent her pulse pounding. And after the first encounter, he hadn't spoken. Maybe he thought she wasn't worth the effort.

Or maybe he'd spoken before thinking. Maybe he would have apologized for what he'd said if she hadn't rushed in with the 'you're rude' tantrum. Well, it didn't matter now. Thinking about him anymore wasn't a good use of time.

Yet Laura's mind refused to listen to common sense. Try as she might, she couldn't get him off her mind. From anger to attraction, she fought with her emotions.

Inside the house, she let the dogs off their leashes. Sophia trotted to her bed without even the decency to act sorry for charging away. She'd have to keep the two on a tighter rein next time. Laura set the kettle to boil, deciding a nice hot cup of tea would be good. She'd treat herself tonight and head back to the White Swan for dinner.

The rest of the day passed in quiet compared to the morning's outing. Dressing in a soft Merino sweater and brown slacks, she added a scarf that complimented the cream and tan palette. Slipping into her trench coat, she checked her reflection in the mirror. She'd styled her hair up into a French twist, adding some pearls. She stared into the mirror and spoke.

"No. Stop being a wimp!" She imagined her book club ladies who'd all come to see her off on her trip. Their admonitions of 'have fun' and 'take chances' still rang in her memory.

Had Deneuve or other celebrities ever faced the same doubts she felt? It didn't matter. She rarely ate out alone at home. Here she was going to go out to dinner alone in a strange new city. Perhaps it would be better to stay in and eat the premade dinner she'd bought from Tesco.

She walked over to the pub and up the steps. Taking a deep breath, she said, "New strong, independent woman. You can do this." Laura opened the door.

Chapter Three

Surprising Rescue

Inside, the warmth of the interior hit her. Conversations and general restaurant noise accosted her. The pub was packed. Dark wooden beams aged from time crossed the ceiling and some spots along the wall, creating a snug feeling. It hadn't seemed this busy when Lavinia and her husband had brought her last time. Or had it been because she was with them and felt more comfortable? She didn't see any unoccupied tables. Her bravado at dining solo fizzled.

She turned to see a group of men laughing and joking. Before she could look away, one man caught her eye. "Hey, Luv. Need a seat? You can sit next to me." He patted the oak chair next to him.

A waitress brushed by with pints of yeasty beer and a plate of fried fish and mushy peas.

Her throat grew dry. How could she respond without causing a scene? She struggled with her response when from behind her, a smooth voice like velvet came to her ears.

"Hello, love. I already have our table."

Laura swiveled to see the man from this afternoon. "You!"

"May I?" He crooked his arm. She had to make a decision. And now. She placed her hand on his tweed jacket as she glanced back at the men.

The men laughed and moaned, clutching at their chests, "Ah, next time, Luv!" They went back to their pints. She smiled at their joking. If nothing else, it had given her a bit of a confidence boost.

She stole a glance at the man from earlier today. Up close he retained his handsome features. Allowing him to escort her, he led her to a corner table tucked into a quieter alcove. Cozy, with wood paneling on two sides, it created a pleasant spot. Now she had to decide to stay or go. Her stomach rumbled and she hoped it hadn't been loud enough for him to hear.

He gestured to her coat. "May I help you with that?"

Should she? He waited so she slid her arms from her coat, and he hung it on a hook next to his. Laura's mind raced as he pulled out the chair for her, and she tried to think of a way out of her predicament. Waiting for him to take his seat, she stole glances at his chiseled jaw and a faint outline of beard growth. A strange sensation of wanting to reach up and touch his jaw surprised her. She forced herself to look at her lap, wringing her hands to get rid of the tension inside.

He must have been some looker when he was younger. Who are you kidding? He's got movie star looks now.

"First, introductions. My name is Hugh—"

Before she could answer, a waitress appeared. "Sir, may I get you something to drink?"

"Pinot Grigio, please." His gaze toward her made her mouth go dry. Beyond a doubt, he had a strange effect on her. How could she get up and leave without causing another scene? The words from her book club friends jumped into her mind. Take a chance, right?

"I'll have the same. Thank you."

They remained quiet after the woman had left. She broke the silence. "I'm Laura. I appreciate your coming to my aid earlier."

"Well, it would have been 'rude' for me not to come to the defense of a lady." His vowels were crisp and very much the received pronunciation like the late Queen spoke. All Laura knew was that his dialect screamed upper crust.

"About that—"She was cut off from saying anything else before their server reappeared with their wine.

"Sir." She set his drink down in front of Hugh before placing the wine glass before Laura.

He waited until the lady had left before saying in his charming English, "You were saying?"

"I realized after I thought about it for a bit that I had misunderstood you." She hated having to admit it, but it had been later that afternoon when she realized he'd been talking about Sophia. She laughed at her stupidity, thankful she wouldn't have the humiliation of being called out about it. And yet here she was now. Eating crow. Or whatever would be the English equivalent.

"Go on." She gazed into understanding gray eyes that held some humor in them. The rat. He was enjoying watching her squirm.

"I was so intent on getting Sophia ... well, it didn't dawn on me you were talking about the dog. I want to apologize for my rudeness."

"Accepted. One should never assume."

She bristled at his statement.

"Did I offend you again?"

"No, it's just something I hear often from my daughter."

"You have children?"

"Yes." Laura noticed he stole a glance at her left hand, which still bore her wedding band. "I have one daughter and grandkids that keep me busy. And two sons. Though they don't live close, I don't get to see them as much. What about you?"

"What about me?"

"I mean, do you have children?"

"No." His clipped tone bore no more questioning in that area.

Laura sipped at the dry, light-bodied wine. *This is going to be a long night if that's the extent of his answers.*

Laura looked around the pub at the other diners, anywhere but at the man across from her. Her hands twisting together under the table. What was it about him that made her feel self-conscious?

His gaze focused on her as he said, "Why are you here?"

"I came here the other night. I enjoyed it, and since it's close, well, I thought I'd come back and eat here again." Stop the babbling, Laura. She clamped her mouth closed.

His upturned lips let Laura know that wasn't what he meant.

"Oh, geez. I did it again. Sorry, I misunderstood you."

"Do you apologize for everything, or is it just to me?"

She looked at her lap. "No, it's just that, well, can I be honest?"

"Have you not been honest thus far?"

She noted the upturn of his lips as she continued, "I'm like a fish out of water here. I've never traveled abroad. John and I were going to travel when he retired. It never happened. So here I am, not understanding about chains in the bathrooms and stoves with no knobs, and... It doesn't matter. I'm rambling."

"So you're married—"

"Was." The statement hung in the air as their eyes met and held. Like the park all over again. She wanted to look away but couldn't. Neither spoke. Yet so much passed between them.

Their server came over and asked if they'd like to order any food. He responded. "I'll be staying for dinner, too. If that is acceptable to you." His glance at Laura caused her heart to do a little somersault. Just wait until the Book Club ladies hear about this.

"Certainly."

"Would you like me to order for us?"

The words 'take a chance' echoed in her mind. "Okay."

Please, oh please don't order anything that had stomach contents or worse in it before now.

He spoke to the waitress. "We'll have the Sunday joint, with bubble and squeak." Facing Laura, he asked, "Are you up for some spotted dick?"

A flush went up Laura's neck. She forced back a laugh before clearing her throat. "Uh, say again?"

"Don't worry. You'll love it." He spoke to the server as Laura composed herself. She bit her lip to stop the laughter. How old was she? Nine?

She heard him say, "We'll have that as well. With coffee."

Oh, thank heavens. It must be a dessert. Not some part that would emerge on her plate. It was difficult to look and act sophisticated when everything in the country made her giggle like a schoolgirl.

"If you'll excuse me, I'm going to go to the powder room and wash my hands before dinner."

He rose as she did, pulling her chair away from the table.

"Thank you."

In the bathroom, she took a moment to think about her situation. Here she was, dining with a handsome man with impeccable manners. She felt a bit giddy with it. Now she had to stop giggling about foods with anatomy names. Swiping her rose lipstick on her lips, she glanced at the mirror. A woman of newfound veracity stood watching her. She patted her hair as another woman joined her at the mirror.

"That's a wonderful color on you."

"Thank you." How long had it been since she'd been complimented for her looks? What was it about older women that turned them invisible? She hadn't cared for a long time. Now within a short amount of time, first the flight attendant and now this lady had complimented her. Renewed confidence flowed through her. Is that what it was?

She took a deep breath and exited the bathroom. Arriving back at the table she saw that Hugh wasn't there. She glanced at the coat rack. The hook where his jacket had been was now empty.

She groaned. So much for a polite English gentleman. Rude would still be an accurate term for him. Instead, a world-class jerk came to mind. Now she'd be stuck paying for two meals and drinks.

He must have been thrilled when she left so he could make his escape. She stiffened at the rebuff and took a moment to collect herself. She let out a cleansing breath. So what? His loss. And bonus, she could take the extra food back for a meal tomorrow. She would refuse to let one man ruin her evening.

She sensed his presence as warmth radiated toward her. A rich male scent followed as he came up behind her. She moved her head as he whispered close to her ear, "I do apologize. I decided to take the opportunity as well."

Laura accepted his pulling out of her chair, glad to sit as her knees weakened. Finding her equilibrium, she replied, "You took your coat with you?"

"Yes. I have some important documents in here. As well as my wallet." He patted his jacket breast pocket. "You had taken your handbag with you, and I believed your coat to be safe. If not, I apologize for not waiting. I didn't want to disturb our conversation. Most ladies tend to take some time in the lounge, so I believed I could pop over and back before you returned."

"Maybe English ladies. Or ladies who like to primp. I've never been one to do that much."

"Nor would you need to."

Laura swallowed. Sylvie's ministrations on getting her brows waxed and dyed, along with adding some lowlights to her hair, had paid off. Other than a flick of mascara and her new lipstick, her face bore only moisturizer and a blusher color stick she'd applied. Trying to hide her embarrassment, she pulled her napkin into her lap.

The server came over, setting their meals in front of them. "May I get you anything else, sir?"

He addressed Laura. "Do you have everything you need, love?"

"Um, yes. Thank you." She knew the term 'love' was used another way than in American lingo, but it still sent a shiver up her spine. How long ago it had been when she'd last heard those words? Sadness crept in.

Oh, John. Why did you leave me?

"Is everything satisfactory?" His warm gaze met hers again.

"Yes, thank you. Everything looks delicious." She watched as he cut a piece of the cooked meat with his left hand. He held his fork with the tines turned down. "I forget that we even have differences when it comes to the way we hold our cutlery."

"One should try it our way. It makes the most sense."

Laura nodded, using her left hand to cut a piece of meat, and turning the fork upside down. It felt strange in her hand, but taking chances didn't have to mean important things. It could be as simple as trying to do something you did all the time in a different way. Like using your opposite hand to brush your teeth or putting your coat on with the opposite arm first. It's supposed to add new paths in the brain which couldn't hurt the older she got.

His voice interrupted her thoughts. He smiled, kindness radiating from his eyes. Her formal demeanor melted.

"There you have it. You've done a bang-up job. We'll make a Brit of you yet."

A flush crept across her cheeks.

Chapter Four

Unexpected Connection

During the delightful meal, Laura enjoyed the medley of buttery potatoes and cabbage in the Bubble and Squeak. It complemented the meat. She learned Hugh had been attending to some business in London. They shared pleasantries about things strangers feel are safe to discuss. They'd moved on to their odd-named dessert which turned out to be a steamed pudding with dried fruit. It was accompanied by a side of creamy sweet custard. As it was set down in front of them, hints of vanilla along with other sweet fragrances wafted from the dessert. They had poured some of the custard over their dessert as the waitress brought their coffees.

Taking a bite, she moaned, "Ummm, this is so good." She realized the sounds she'd made and looked to see his gaze fixed on her. Thankfully, a loud crash as a chair fell over broke the spell.

He sat back and asked, "I believe one didn't get the answer to what brings you to us."

Laura couldn't help the giggle that escaped. She'd heard the term one used versus I with the British. However, this was the first time it had been spoken directly to her. She pulled her napkin up to compose herself. She didn't want to be rude or appear foolish in front of him. She set her coffee cup on the table. She wiped her mouth before answering. "I'm in a book club, and we each had to pick a book from a different genre. I was assigned historical fiction. So I picked one set here."

He leaned forward, "Let me guess. Pride and Prejudice?"

Laura chuckled. "No. Though I considered Austen's books. No, it's Rebecca by Daphne du Maurier. The book also had to be a classic. Plus, who doesn't love a good romance with a mystery?"

"Interesting choice. I thought you might share one of the bodice rippers."

She broke eye contact, stumbling over her words. "No, no, that's not for me. The ladies and I are all past the bodice-ripping stage. I mean—"

Geez, why had she said that? Her face flushed, and a rush of heat went to her cheeks and neck. She cleared her throat, trying to think of something else to say. "I mean, we're more mature ladies that enjoy more cerebral reading. Though we don't mind—"

Ack, shut up, Laura! You're only digging a deeper hole. "Is it me or is it a bit warm in here?" She adjusted her scarf with her hands.

His pursed lips revealed his amusement at her statements. She reached for the creamer with shaky hands.

He did the same and their fingers brushed each other. She drew back quickly but not before tingles rose in her fingers. Get a grip, Laura.

Most times, this stumbling over her words wouldn't be an issue, but something about Hugh unnerved her. With a jolt, it came to her.

He was listening. To her. Really listening. Asking questions. Having someone's complete attention was so rare that Laura envisioned a spotlight shining on her. She wasn't sure if she liked it or not. He didn't speak to fill the silence but waited for her to continue.

Setting her cup down, she moved forward on to a new subject. "Anyway, it got me interested in the history of the country. I discovered a fictional account of Henry the Eighth."

"So, you came here to see where King Henry lived?"

She nodded, enthusiasm in her voice. "The story intrigued me, and I knew some of my ancestors came from here, so I did some searching. I've found some names and thought it would be fun to come check it out. My friend, Betsy found me this pet sit so here I am."

"Ah, so you're a hire."

Laura stiffened. Did he just demote her? She refrained from a catty response.

"No. it's a trade. I stay in their home, which gives me time to explore the area, and they leave me to care for their pets. I'm not a 'hire' or whatever you called it."

"My apologies, madam. I meant no offense. Would you like a glass of port to finish our meal?"

"I'm not sure—" Laura fiddled with her napkin, unable to understand the assault of emotions inside. She brushed her hair back away from her face.

"It helps with digestion. Plus, it means we can continue our conversation."

She pressed her lips together as her insides quivered. It'd been so long that any man had flirted with her. Was he flirting or simply being nice? It was so much easier when she didn't have to ponder every word or gesture. His gaze rested on her and she struggled to look away.

"Okay. That sounds nice."

"What places have you visited thus far?" Hugh asked.

"Mostly around here. The dogs already have a walker a few times a week, so that's the time I can spend more time away from the house. I plan to go to Kensington Palace. I've been to the Tower of London, Westminster Abbey, and some other downtown sights. I enjoy walking around, admiring the architecture, and listening to all the accents. There's so much to see here. I doubt I'll get to see everything before I leave."

"May I be so bold as to inquire when that is?"

"Another couple of weeks." She stopped speaking when the server brought the goblets with the dark, rich liquid. She sipped the strong port.

"A few weeks? What a tragedy. Now, you must let me help you with your ancestor's search. Do you have any paperwork on it?"

"Yes. But I don't have it with me. It's back at the house."

"Did you bring your car or take a taxi?"

"No, I walked." Laura didn't give out info to strangers. Remember that guy called Jack the Ripper? Should she make up something?

"I believe I may be able to help you with your research. May I join you and retrieve the papers? I can assist you in your pursuit since your time here is limited."

Laura hesitated. His offer would be helpful, but what did she know about this man? Nothing at all. She knew some men preyed on lonely, old women. She didn't want to fall into that trap. If her emotions all evening were any indication of her attraction to him, he'd be foolish not to pick up on some of it. Yet she felt comfortable and safe with him. Of course, that's what the lady sitting next to Bundy at the phone bank had said.

Oh geez. She had to say something. He stared at her, his eyes dropping to her lips. Waiting for an answer.

Or something else? Then it dawned on her. "I'm sorry. As you can imagine, I can't allow anyone into their home."

"Understandable. I will wait outside on the steps for you to retrieve the papers. I wouldn't be so bold as to ask a lady I just met to invite me into her home."

Laura had run out of excuses. "Well, okay. Now, do we pay here at the table, or do we need to go up to the counter?"

"The meal is accounted for. I appreciated the company. One can only dine alone so much."

She smiled while listening to him. Even though it was the same language, she reveled in the way he spoke. His formal phrasing reminded her she was in a different country. "I could at least pay for the tip."

"Unnecessary. Are you ready to depart?"

She nodded, and he came around and pulled the chair back so she could rise. Taking her coat from the hook, he held it open for her before putting his jacket on. His movements were so gentle, yet manly. She should have looked away, but she couldn't. The strangest desire to reach out and touch his face jolted her. It had been decades since she'd experienced such attraction to a man. It left her confused and ungrounded.

Their eyes met and for a moment, the world faded away. Someone hitting a chair nearby broke the spell. He stood back and directed her to go forward with his hand. Should she feel at least a bit guilty she'd stolen a glance at his left hand. Of course, some married men didn't wear a ring.

Chills went up her spine. With a light touch on the small of her back, he steered her toward the door. Warmth rose in Laura's body. Even John had never treated her with such deference. She could get used to this. Shocked at her thoughts, she focused on the pub's exit.

"Good night, sir. Madam." The waitress came to clear their table.

"Do you dine here often? It seemed like that server knew you."

"Yes. I frequent this pub when I'm in town."

That explained it then. Plus, she called him sir a lot. She stole a glance at him. Was he a real Sir versus just the name given to a man? No way to ask without being impolite.

They stepped out into the chilly night air, he crooked his arm for her to take. "Shall we?"

Deciding to accept the offer, she threaded her arm through his. As they drew together, the warmth of his body radiated into her own. "It's just a block over."

"Lead on, madam." His smile loosened the tension in her shoulders.

As they strolled, Hugh regaled her with the history of the homes where the aristocratic set and monied lived in the past.

The wealthy still do today she thought. After she'd arrived, she'd looked up the townhouse where she was staying. The price listed the home in the tens of millions. She'd whistled on seeing its value.

Arriving at the house, she removed her arm from his. "This is it."

"I will remain here on the pavement."

"Okay. It may take a minute. Are you sure? It's cold out here."

"All's well." He gave a slight bow.

She took the set of marble steps up to the door while Hugh remained behind. Unlocking the door, she turned to see him staring at her. She gave a quick wave before entering the two-story hallway. As a creature of habit, she turned the lock on the door behind her. She made her way up the stairs to her room, where she glanced in a nearby mirror.

"Hey, taking a chance, remember?"

Pulling the papers from the desk in an alcove, she patted her hair where a few tendrils had come loose. She'd left her purse downstairs in her haste to get the paper. So much for being able to freshen her face or touch up her lipstick.

What are you thinking, Laura? It's not like he's going to kiss you.

The idea of Hugh kissing her made Laura pause. She needed to get her head on straight. It had to be the new environment, coupled with the wine, and heavy food. Add that all together, plus the port must be putting such baffling thoughts into her mind.

Forcing herself not to race down the stairs, she made it to the front door. Opening it, she spied Hugh pacing back and forth. Even though he wore heavy brown gloves, with his fists clenched. He blew into his hands making her sorry she'd kept him waiting in the cold. Upon seeing her, he came up the steps.

She handed him the paper. "This is what I have."

He took it from her, looking at the various notes. "May I keep this? I will return it to you without delay."

She shrugged. "I suppose. I do have a copy on my computer."

"Wonderful. Now may I be so daring as to ask for a number where I may reach you?"

She rattled off her cell phone number as he plugged it into his phone. He typed a few lines and then hit send. "There. Now you have my number as well." He bundled the papers into his jacket before moving down one step.

Laura stuck out her hand for him to shake. "Thank you for a lovely dinner."

"The pleasure was all mine." He took her hand and pressed his lips to it. "Until we meet again." He trotted down the other steps as agile as a much younger man, striding off before turning back to wave good night.

Hesitating to move, the cold breeze impressed Laura to return to the warm interior. She locked the door and stared down at her hand.

"Sorry, Hugh. But the pleasure was all mine."

Chapter Five

Second Chance

Waking to warm sunlight streaming through tall windows, Laura stretched her arms overhead. She snuggled into the bed linens, the previous evening's memories still lingering.

Her friends would be proud. She'd more than taken a chance. She'd had dinner with a handsome man she'd just met. A perfect stranger. Oh, and yes, he had been perfect. After she'd decided he wasn't a stalker or serial killer. If she could have conjured up her own dream man, it would be hard-pressed not to have been Hugh.

Handsome, gentlemanly, and best of all, listening to her.

When he kissed her hand, everything had ceased around her. His touch had sent a shiver through her. Who even did that in this day and age? It was something from ... what was it he called them? Oh, yeah, bodice rippers. Or Austen's time. Not in the twenty-first century. So he was old school. All she knew was he'd made her feel like a young woman again. Even better, he had gotten her phone number. Wait, he'd sent her a text message last night. She'd been so flustered over the kiss and letting the dogs out into the garden, she'd forgotten.

Springing from her bed, she scurried over to where her phone sat on the charger.

When she saw what he had written, she broke out in laughter. It said, "Rude man."

With the dogs off with the regular walker for the day, Laura decided to head to Kensington Palace.

While she'd planned to visit it later, she'd discovered that it had a Princess Diana exhibit with her dresses on display. After dressing and a quick breakfast, she decided to make her way over to take the tour.

The skies may have been gray yesterday, but Laura had a new pep in her step after last night. Oh, how she'd needed the feelings that had long been buried. As if the sun had come out to greet her she stepped outside. Arriving at Kensington, she marveled at the staircase Victoria had taken to learn she was now queen. Taking in the Palace's rooms, she enjoyed learning of its history, and its inhabitants past and present.

Making her way to the exhibit, Laura took her time admiring the beautiful gowns. She recalled the late princess wearing them, but to see them in person made it all real. And sad. After finishing the exhibit, she made her way outside. Her thoughts drifted back in time to the fairytale wedding that had ended in disaster. And it made her mind wander back to her marriage.

Far from perfect, as any marriage is, it had been comfortable. So when they'd received the horrible diagnosis, it had come as a shock to them both. Their long-anticipated travels had turned into trips to the doctor's offices, staying at home to care for an ever frailer and ailing body, and neglecting her health and well-being.

She wiped at the tears that had sprung to her eyes. Even after all this time, little things would set her off. And maybe always would. Well, at least those days are long behind me. Now I'm granny, and my days of marriage and all it entails are done.

Even as she thought the words, her heart pinched at never sharing the love of a husband, companionship, friendship, and dare she even think it, sex again. The mere idea of displaying a "closed" shop sign on a placard hanging from her neck sent her pulse racing.

Last night her pulse raced. But due to feeling alive and attractive. Visible.

More and more she'd felt as if she'd been wearing a cloak of invisibility due to her age in certain social situations. John always said her beauty turned men's heads. Nowadays, no one's head turned or even acknowledged her. Or not that she'd known.

Yet, Sylvie had helped her come out of her style slump. The woman convinced the entire book club to be her guinea pigs for being a stylist. She'd pegged Laura as a classic beauty and whisked her off to the hairdressers for a fresh cut and color. A simple make-up palette had brought oohs and aahs from the ladies in the salon.

As she strolled through the sunken gardens, her mind wandered back in time. And the one dress Sylvie had insisted Laura buy in particular. Sylvie had put together a day for them to try on clothes at a local boutique. Laura never entered the 'bougie' place before, but Sylvie insisted. She'd promised to help Laura pick out some clothing for travel. The rest of the ladies had come along to have fun too.

The store had closed earlier, leaving the women with glasses of Prosecco. The laughter flowed as the women tried on dresses. Sylvie had appeared at Laura's dressing room with a cobalt gown draped over her arm. Composed of beautiful velvet with lace along the bodice top and sleeves, it was a beautiful dress. Laura immediately fell in love with it.

Laura stared at the gown. "I won't ever wear something like that."

"Hogwash!" Betsy appeared at Sylvie's side, holding up a teal pantsuit. "Look at what she's got me trying on. This is our time to stop saying no and start saying 'yes' to new experiences. Plus, that dress looks like it was made for you."

"See? If Betsy says you need to try it on, then you must." Sylvie handed the dress over to Laura and shooed her off to the dressing room.

Laura ran her hand over the soft velvet. Could something feel like luxury? Because this did. She held it up in front of her. They were right. The rich, vibrant color a perfect complement to her skin tones and hair color.

"When you have it on, come out so we can see you in it!" Betsy hollered through the closed dressing room door.

Taking the dress from the hanger, she stepped into it. Pulling it up, it slid over her womanly curves. Though she had to admit she was thankful it had a side zipper. When she closed it, she stared at the reflection in the mirror. The dress fit her like a glove. She turned sideways, admiring the woman in the mirror. She twisted back and forth by the mirror, her face beaming.

After more cajoling from the other ladies, she walked to the boutique's lounge.

Sylvie gasped and ran over to greet her. "Oh. You're stunning! That dress was made for you."

The others agreed.

"How do you feel?" asked Francis.

"I, well, I—"

"Out with it!" Betsy cajoled.

"I feel beautiful." The words came out in a whisper.

"As you should. You are beautiful," Sylvie responded.

The others chimed in, agreeing with her.

"You must buy this dress!"

"Sylvie, there's nowhere I'll ever wear it." She glanced at the price tag, shocked to see it cost more than a thousand dollars.

Sylvie folded her arms, tapping her heeled foot on the floor. "Let me ask you something, Laura, and I want you to be honest with us. When was the last time you bought anything for yourself that wasn't a need but a want? I'll wait."

Laura glanced at the other woman who awaited her response. The truth was, she hadn't even bought anything that had made her heart sing like this dress did. It had been forever. Or if she was honest, even at all. Her bras and panties had been on sale, items that did the job, not those silk ones she ran her hands across as she shopped. After John died, it wasn't like she needed to have anything decorative or sexy, so she'd stayed with utilitarian.

As if she had read her mind, Sylvie said, "I bet you don't even allow yourself beautiful lingerie. Why?"

Laura shrugged, "No one's going to see it."

"You're going to see it! You are worth it, and you need to make yourself happy."

Francis laughed, "Sylvie, I didn't know you were taking us out for therapy sessions."

Sylvie threw back her head laughing. "Hey, that could be on my business card. One Stop Shopping and Therapy! Look good and feel good."

She held up her glass and all the ladies clinked their glasses with hers. "To therapy!"

Once their laughter had died down, Francis spoke to Laura. "Listen, I understand. When you don't have someone at home, you think, *What's the point*? But it's important. And seriously, that dress is so you. It should be called the Laura dress."

Shirley, ever the pragmatic one, replied, "Here's the real question. Can you afford it?"

Laura nodded. Truth was John had left her with no debt and a substantial pension.

"Then buy it!" The group chimed.

"Okay, okay!" She held up her hands in surrender as she sashayed back to the dressing room. She had kept the dress and on a whim had brought it with her on the trip.

It still bore the price tag.

Chapter Six

Romance in the Air

Back at the townhouse, Laura ordered an Indian curry for dinner. It was fun hearing it shared as a takeaway instead of to-go like in the States. Those minor differences made Laura smile. The curry had been filling and delightful with its spices of cumin and ginger on her tastebuds. The dish had enough heat with the coconut milk added to make it fit her palate. She even had enough for tomorrow's lunch, along with some naan she'd saved to go with it.

She settled in before a warm fire, book in hand, and the dogs nearby on a fluffy bed. She sighed with contentment. I could get used to this.

She laid the book in her lap, her thoughts drifting. Why did she need to get used to anything? She was beholden to no one but herself. When had she given up simple things like starting a fire? Or anything that felt like luxury without feeling a need to admonish herself over it? Days were often spent doing things around the house. Even exercising had become another chore to check off her daily to-do list.

Laura gazed around the room with its overstuffed chairs, begging to call you to sit. Prints and other artwork dotted the room from their travels, most likely bringing back good memories of their trips. Under her feet, a thick Persian rug caused her to shuck her slippers whenever she sat there, enjoying the feel of its heft under her feet. So different from her own contemporary garden home.

As John neared retirement, they'd downsized. While she enjoyed her smaller house, it had never felt like home. Had the lack of decorating been a signal that she hadn't made any effort? A feeling of unease had settled over it like a dark cloud as if the house retained all the medical comings and goings. John's illness had left its mark on the house as much as her.

First, nurses had come once a week, and then daily visits, but later, the guest room had been reconfigured. Everything was moved out so the medical bed could be brought in. John insisted on that, as he didn't want their master bedroom in upheaval. Days and nights she spent at his bedside. Nothing else existed. Or mattered.

Later it changed to hours and minutes. After the hospice nurse had left the room, John reached up with a frail hand, pulling her to him.

"You know I will love you to my last breath. Which looks like it's coming pretty soon." He laughed, but it turned into a coughing fit. He waved away her attempts to help him. "I need you to promise me something."

"Anything."

"I want you to be open to love."

"John—" She shook her head.

"I'm serious, darling. You have so much love to give. You give to the point where you don't receive. There are so many gifts I wanted to give you. So many places we were going to see. Now I won't be able to do that. But someone else can."

"Please, let's not talk about this."

"It needs to be said. I don't want you to give up your dreams. Travel, meet new people, love again." He winced as the pain hit him.

She stood, wanting to flee from the conversation. "I'll get the nurse."

"And don't let Caroline run over you. I love my daughter, but you are not to be at her beck and call."

Laura laughed. "Okay. I will."

But she hadn't.

She'd merely gone along with whatever was needed. Even though the house felt cold and empty without John, she struggled to move forward.

She'd put off redecorating.

She'd put off traveling.

She'd put off living.

The book slid off her lap, falling to the floor. Sophia and Gregory raised their heads as if to question her.

"It's okay, guys." She picked up her book and laid it on the table next to her. Using the remote, she clicked on the television going over to where music could be played. She clicked and the song, Everybody Hurts started.

Geez really? It was one of John's favorite songs. Tears fell as she listened to the heart-wrenching words. They turned to laughter as she recalled them dancing in the kitchen after his diagnosis. They'd cried, then laughed, and then made love. He'd joked he wanted to be with her as long as he could.

Thank you, thank you, John.

She smiled at the memory. She could hold on. Even better, she was ready to move forward.

Why had this all come to mind? Maybe because she didn't feel at home in her own house. A new place would be the fresh start she needed. This trip might serve as the impetus she needed to break out from her rut. When she got home, she might look for other places. For now, she could enjoy dreaming.

She rose and found her laptop. Once logged in, she pulled up a site with houses for sale. Ooh, wouldn't it be lovely to design her own home? One with a fireplace, for sure. Possibly in the Colorado mountains up by Estes Park or Glenwood. Of course, that wouldn't work with helping with the kids.

Why are you holding back from what you want?

Setting her teacup on the nearby coaster, she picked up her book. Laura liked it that the ladies had come together and named the chosen books. This way everyone knew in advance what book they were reading. She'd be returning home before they met again, but they had a backup where they'd teleconference if needed.

Her phone rang, and she smiled to see Hugh's name on the screen. "Hello, Hugh."

"Good evening. I hope I am not imposing. If needs must, I can call back at a later time."

"No. This works." She snuggled into the cushy pillows and pulled the soft fleece wrap over her feet and legs.

"Brilliant. I spoke with someone who helped me to root out your ancestry."

Laura sat forward, her heart leaping at the news. "Yes?"

"It turns out that one of your ancestors, Lady Jane Collingsworth was named as one lady-in-waiting at Hampton Court."

"Really! How fun is that?" Laura held the phone tighter. "Hopefully not to one of Henry's six wives. I hope she didn't end up in the Tower."

Hugh's melodious voice carried through the line. "No, but she is listed as being one lady at court during that time."

"Well, who knew? Thanks for finding that out for me. I appreciate it."

There was a brief silence on the line.

Laura glanced at the phone to see if they were still connected. She placed the phone by her ear. "Hello? Hugh?"

"If I may be so bold, might I accompany you to view Hampton Court? In addition to its being where your ancestors lived, I think you will find the architecture intriguing."

"Oh, I'd like that. I have a full day off next week on Tuesday when the dogs go to the groomers."

"Splendid."

Laura shifted her position. "Great. Do you want to meet here or at the train station?"

"Train station?"

"Yes, I purchased a senior pass when I came over. It saved me quite a bit of money. Do you have one?"

"No."

Laura babbled on, "It's easy. I did splurge for the first-class section, but I'm willing to sit in the regular area if needed."

There was another brief pause before he replied, "Why ever not? I can meet you at your house and we can walk over together. Would nine o'clock suit?"

"Yes, that sounds perfect."

"Until next week then."

"Till next week. Bye." Laura ended the call, smiling to herself. Okay, so this time he'd asked her to go somewhere with him. Did that constitute being a date? Either way, it didn't matter. Being able to spend more time with this thoughtful, handsome man was good enough. She sprang up from the couch and did a little twirl. Stopping, she noticed the dogs looking up at her.

"What? You've never seen a giddy American before?"

Tuesday couldn't come fast enough for Laura. She spent her days caring for and walking the dogs. At night, she curled up with her book club read in front of the fire. She'd settled in with her book when her phone chirped. She picked it up and looked at the screen.

Betsy had written, All good? How do you like pet sitting?

Love it. I wish I had known about this before. The people are so nice.

Yes, when I pet-sat for them, it is one of the best sits I've done. Also, a terrific location.

Laura typed. Well, I appreciate your helping me with this.

Any luck with finding any information about your ancestors?

Yes. I met a man who is helping me with it. Laura replied.

Oh, do tell. Maybe he's a duke or something.

I met him out walking one day. Plus you know there are only thirty dukes? Of non-royals, only twenty-four dukedoms. For some reason, romance writers always choose a duke for their love interest.

Betsy replied. I don't keep up much with romances but interesting. So how'd you meet this guy?

Laura related the incident to the misunderstanding. Betsy replied with a laughing emoji.

Sounds like something I'd do.

I saw him again at a pub that's close by. He already had a table, so he asked if I'd like to join him for dinner.

Wow emojis graced her screen.

Laura typed. It's nothing like that. He's a nice guy. That's all.

Nice guys are good to have around. Not that I care, but what about the looks department?

Distinguished. Good dresser. A gentleman.

All good, but what does he look like?

Laura thought for a moment before typing.

Handsome. Tall. Auburn hair but with some silver. More on his sideburns. I hate that men look so distin-guished with their gray. Yet us women look like we've aged twenty years. Not fair.

Betsy shot back with a line of starry eye emojis. Silver Fox, huh?

Laura laughed as another text came through.

Remind you of anybody?

Hmmm. Laura thought about Hugh. Hard to say, but maybe a combination of Christopher Plummer and Timothy Dalton.

Wowzer. He is a looker!!!

Laura chuckled before typing. Yes, he is.

When will you be seeing him again?

Next week. We're traveling out to tour Hampton Court. Where my ancestors may have lived.

Very cool.

Yes, it is.

Well, dogs here are giving me the stink eye for their walk. Keep me posted!

Will do.

Laura set her phone down and scooted down on the sofa. She opened her book again when another chime sounded on her phone.

It was another text message from Betsy.

Don't forget our book club mantra. She finished it with a smiley face.

How could she forget? It felt like every day since she'd joined the book club, there had been a constant 'take a chance' refrain. So what if she'd be leaving soon, and never see Hugh again? It felt good to be appreciated as a person and as a woman. His attention had made her feel attractive after such a long time feeling unnoticed. No more. She'd enjoy every minute of this trip. Especially Tuesday.

***

Tuesday arrived. Laura struggled with deciding what to wear for the outing. She tried on various outfits before discarding each. At home, she'd have grabbed a shirt and jeans, but she wanted to make a good impression. She had better stop her indecision, or she'd be in her bathrobe when Hugh arrived. She settled on a navy top with navy slacks and matching comfortable walking shoes. She left her hair loose in a wavy blowout from yesterday's stop at a local salon. Adding a pair of pearl earrings she pulled a silk scarf from her accessories, adding a lightweight addition to her outfit. Topping off her makeup with a swipe of coral lipstick, she headed downstairs to wait for Hugh to arrive.

She had just finished drinking her hot coffee with cream when the front doorbell sounded.

Speaking to the dog, she said, "Gregory, please get that for me, won't you?"

The dog cocked his head to suggest, 'What did you say?'

"Okay, fine. But you're a lousy butler." She pet his head as she made her way to the door.

When she opened the door, Hugh turned to face her, a small bouquet in his hand. "I passed this shoppe on my way here. They reminded me of you." He held them out to her.

"That's thoughtful. Thank you." She took the mixed floral bouquet and held the door wider for him to enter.

"Am I allowed inside?"

Laura smiled, "Yes, I asked, and they said it was fine. Just no sleepovers." She stopped, realizing what she'd said. Heat rose in her chest "Um, I mean. Other guests. Um, I'll just put these in water." She strode away before he could see the redness she felt coursing up her neck and the flush on her cheeks.

Finding a glass vase, she poured water into it before adding the stems to the water. "I will cut those, but I can do that later."

"We have time if you'd like to do that now."

"Okay." She turned away but tingling rose in her limbs. No doubt he was watching her as she sensed his eyes on her. She dropped the scissors. Retrieving them from the sink, she cut off a stem, and it dropped to the floor. She had become so clumsy and self-conscious with him so near. He came over and picked it up.

"Here you go, love."

She swallowed. Where had this unsure teenage girl come from and where had the mature woman she knew gone?

"It may behoove us to work in tandem. May I cut the stems and you can arrange them?"

"Good idea."

Working side by side, they made quick work of the floral arrangement, and Laura placed them on the kitchen table. "They're gorgeous. Thank you for these. I love flowers."

"You're welcome. Shall we go?"

"Yes." She reached for the jacket on the chair, but he found it first. He held it open as he'd done at the pub the other evening. So it wasn't a one-off. He retained the manners of a gentleman. In her younger days, the constant mantra of being independent and do things yourself had pushed this lovely chivalry to the back corner. She could still be an independent woman and enjoy being cared for by an attentive man. She enjoyed this feeling of being special.

His hands stayed a few seconds longer on her shoulders, causing yet one more shiver up her spine. Composing herself, she turned around and faced him. Their eyes met, and electricity surged between them. Or was it just her? Her attraction to him was unlike anything she'd ever experienced. Not even with John. There was this strange feeling, like their souls knew each other. Had been searching for each other. She'd heard people experiencing the feeling before, but this was the first time it had ever happened to her.

Neither moved. Their breath shallow, heavy with anticipation. Struggling to move, she looked away first. "I'll just get my gloves and purse."

He nodded, stepping back from her. She noted the pulsing of his hands into fists to relieve tension. So it wasn't just her.

After exiting and locking the front door, they made their way down the steps to the street.

He crooked his arm, and she laced hers through his. Calm radiated through her. His presence afforded a feeling of safety that came over her as they strolled toward the station. "Were you able to get a ticket?"

"Yes. And we can sit in the first-class section."

"Wonderful. Sometimes it's nice to treat yourself. Don't you think?"

"Yes. Yes, it is." A small smile played on his lips.

They made their way to Kensington Station, the sounds of commuters going and coming catching her ears. They'd arrived in time not to have to hurry before boarding the train to Hampton Court Station. They settled into their seats when Laura spoke. "I enjoy taking the train as we don't have anything like this where I live. We're a car city. Though Denver does have some light rail. Though nothing like the rail system you have here."

She pulled off her gloves and set them next to her purse. "It may take longer, but it's a reminder to slow down and enjoy the moment. And now we'll have time for some conversation before we arrive."

He nodded as she continued. "The other day you said you were visiting London. Do you live close to or a long way from London?"

"My home is in Hampshire."

"Hmm. Sorry, I'm not great at English geography. Is that north or east?"

He pulled out his phone and showed her a map of all the counties. He placed his finger on the map. "My home is close to this area, just outside of Surrey."

"That's a song, I think. Right?"

A bewildered look came to his face.

"Maybe it's an American thing." She smiled as he nodded. They ordered tea and Laura also enjoyed a shortbread biscuit with it. The lemon in the tea and the sweetness of the cookie had a wonderful sweet and tart combination.

They spent the rest of their travel with him pointing out various places or answering Laura's questions. It wasn't long before they pulled into the station. Exiting the train first, Hugh turned and offered Laura his hand. She stepped down from the train, but as if by an unspoken choice, neither one let go. Walking hand in hand, they made their way toward Hampton Court.

Chapter Seven

Blossoming Love

Once they made it to the Hampton Court entrance, she was reluctant to drop his hand. She noticed Hugh cringed a bit when Laura pulled out some pounds to pay for the tickets.

He reached inside his breast pocket for his wallet. "Please permit me."

"You got dinner the other night. I can at least pay for your ticket here." She passed the pounds over to the lady, who gazed at them with a curious expression on her face.

"Only if you will allow me—"

"Let's not start a tit-for-tat between us." She smiled, closing her wallet before placing it back into her purse.

"A what for what?"

They moved away from the counter, his touch light under her forearm.

"You know. You paid for this, so I pay for that, and so on."

"Agreed. From now on, I insist that we have more tats for tats."

She chuckled. "That's not how it goes, but we'll work it out. You've already been so kind by escorting me here and taking time from your busy schedule. It's the least I can do to show my gratitude."

"Why would I not escort a beautiful woman when I have the opportunity?"

Heat rose to her cheeks. Good grief. Being around him gave her more hot flashes than peri-menopause had!

Once the heat dissipated, she glanced at him. His eyes twinkled, but they bore no artifice. His compliment had been sincere. Either that or he was a good liar. She looked away from him to take a moment to compose herself.

Oh, Hugh. Your compliments are water to this thirsty soul.

The large red stone edifice awaited. Best to get her mind focused on that. "Now, since you're the expert, where should we start?"

Hugh shared how the palace construction began under Cardinal Thomas Wolsey. However, after falling out of favor with the King, he gifted the estate to Henry the Eighth.

"Wow. That's some gift."

"Better than losing your head, perhaps?"

"There is that" She put her hands over her eyes and craned her neck back to look up at the magnificent structure.

He continued. "Henry commissioned a substantial enlargement, as he had so many people in his court. One we believe to be your ancestor. From what my friend has ascertained, her husband, Sir Collingsworth, was a knight but died young. It didn't show cause. It could have been during battle or disease. However, Lady Collingsworth remained at Court as a lady-in-waiting."

"Interesting. So who knows? She could have been there when Anne became queen. It's amazing to think about it."

"Yes. I'll share more on the palace's history as we go through to the interior and view the other side, which reflects William's reign."

"Perfect. I appreciate your taking the time today to do this. I hope taking off from work wasn't an issue."

He took a moment to answer her. "All in hand."

Laura realized she must have passed the politeness boundary with her personal questions. She glimpsed a quick intrusion on his face, but it passed by. Must be a touchy subject, so she'd do well to avoid it in the future. Maybe he'd been fired or retired? She glanced at him again. It was hard to determine his age from his youthful looks. But if asking about his job was off-limits, his age would most likely be included.

They strolled through the main gate, Laura arching her neck to take in the stonework and the windows. Moving into the entire courtyard, it was difficult to know where to focus her gaze.

After moving through some interior rooms, they found themselves in the Great Hall. No matter where they walked, they ended up next to one another, as if an invisible cord drew them together if they got too far apart.

"Wow. The beams and the carpentry. Can you imagine all the work that went into this?"

"Yes. Also, you can see Anne still has some memorials here." He pulled her close to him and pointed toward a coat of arms. "There and if you look over here on the ceiling, you can see her falcon emblem."

As Laura gazed at the ceilings adorned with beautiful artwork or architecture, she forced herself to concentrate on the architecture. Instead, his hand at the small of her back garnered her attention. She licked her lips. When she looked down, she found Hugh's gaze on her instead of the surroundings. He quickly looked away but not before she spied confusion and conflict on his face. Had she done or said something to upset him? Or was he feeling the same emotions? She didn't want to read more into it than it was, but it was getting harder.

"Hugh, I hope this isn't too boring for you. I'm sure that you must have been here before."

"Your company is all I require. It's also nice to see your excitement and appreciation for our history."

She blushed. "You English sure have a way with words." Taking his arm, they continued walking through the labyrinth of rooms. They made their way to King Henry's indoor tennis courts.

"This is sure different from what we see today."

"Do you play?"

"No. Though my kids took lessons when they were younger. You?"

Hugh shook his head. "Bad knee stopped my participation in the sport."

"I've heard pickleball is easier. Lots of people are doing it."

"Pickle?"

"It's like tennis, but without all the running around bits. At least that's what I think. If you're ready, should we tour the grounds now?"

"Would you like to stop for elevenses first or wait for lunch?"

Laura stared at Hugh. "I'm sorry. I don't want to appear stupid, but I have no idea what you just asked me."

"Would you like to stop for a coffee or wait and eat luncheon?"

"A coffee break sounds nice. I'm not too hungry, but a biscuit would be nice, too."

He smiled, "You are getting the terminology more and more."

"I'm trying. I want to leave a good impression."

"No need to worry about that. You have."

The pull to rush into his arms overwhelmed her. She'd never been this emotional, even as a teenager. Or at least what she could recall.

"Madam." He crooked his arm, and contentment swept over her with warmth. They'd fallen in sync so easily. How nice to feel cherished and protected by such a simple gesture. They walked to the Tiltyard Café. He held the door open for her.

"What is a Tiltyard?" Laura asked.

"Originally, an enclosed space for jousting."

"You know, it's funny to think that those things went on during those ages. I wonder how many people will marvel at some things we do today?"

"I don't know."

Laura laughed. "I mean … never mind. Are you going to have tea or a coffee?"

"I believe coffee. I don't see this establishment as having a proper cup of tea."

"Okay." She made her way to the counter where Hugh ordered their coffees. Even though the various cookies looked good she recalled having some on the train so she refrained. Taking their drinks outdoors, they sat in quiet for some time, enjoying each other's company.

"I love how the back side of the palace is so different from the front. I am glad William and Mary didn't get the chance to tear it all down, as so much history in the front would have been lost. This is such a treasure."

He sipped at his coffee, listening to her words. "Shall we take a turn around the gardens? I believe we may be getting some rain. I don't believe there are many places to shelter."

"Yes, let's do that. Should we start with the maze?"

A frown appeared on his face before he hid it.

"Ah, come on. I can tell you're not excited about the idea. It'll be fun."

"If you say so."

"Ha! That's an American saying. I think I'm rubbing off on you."

"I gather we're both affecting the other."

Truer words were never spoken.

They spent some time in the maze, finding themselves in dead ends, laughing and starting over. They made their way out and towards the Great Fountain Garden. From there, they would head to the Privy Garden.

They arrived on the long gravel drive from the Great Fountain when light raindrops hit them. He snatched her hand, and they raced forward, laughing all the way. There was no way they'd make it inside. Bolting under a nearby tree, they made it just in time before the heavens opened and rain poured in sheets.

"Isn't it bad to stand under a tree in a storm?" Laura used her scarf to wipe the rain from her face.

"Better than drowning." He gazed down at her. "You're shivering. Come here." He removed his coat and held it over them to add another layer against the cold and rain. She snuggled up to him. The warmth of his body radiated into hers. She laid her cheek against the wool vest he wore. Underneath, his heart pounded. Laura gazed up into his face and their eyes locked. Neither spoke.

Oh, how she wanted him to kiss her. Instead, he dropped one hand from his jacket and rested it gently on her face. She leaned into it, his hand warm against her cheek. Carriage wheels snapped them out of their moment as the large draft horse's hooves clicked on the gravel as it moved past them. The driver steered the beast back down the lane, ferrying tourists to the nearest door.

The spell broken, he commented, "Shall we make a dash for it?"

What she wanted to say was 'No. Let's stay here. Let's stay like this forever. In our own little cocoon away from the world.' Instead, she nodded, "Okay."

Holding his wool coat over their heads, they waited for a reprieve in the downpour before racing toward the doors. Inside, he allowed others to pass by before he hooked his wet coat over his shoulder.

Not even thinking, Laura moved toward him, dusting a kiss on his cheek. "Thank you for taking care of me out there. I mean—"

What had she just done? After John, she'd never kissed another man. Hugs, sure. But not a kiss. And of all the times, to an Englishman who may think she'd overstepped the mark. Isn't that what they said? There was a mark, and you weren't supposed to step over it? Was that—

Ack! Stop it, brain. You're driving me crazy!

She moved back and waited for Hugh to say something. He didn't. Instead, his brow furrowed. Definite conflict there. He took a deep breath to regain his composure. His face grew less stormy in appearance. The upturned corners of his mouth led her to believe no marks had been crossed. Laura forced herself to look away from him.

"Laura?" His voice had grown husky.

"Yes?"

He looked away, his face clouded again. "Nothing."

Chapter Eight

Mixed Messages

Moving away from the door, they found a spot away from others waiting out the rain. The smells of hardwood mingled with the various tones of wet wool and fabrics surrounding them. Staring out the window, Laura wondered what Hugh had wanted to say but hadn't. Maybe she had been reading everything wrong. It wouldn't be the first time some woman had thought a man felt the same way when there was only an offer of friendship. When the weather calmed and the rain moved off they decided to head towards the Privy Garden. As they walked, Laura sensed a shift in the air between them. Maybe she'd made a faux pas and he was trying to hide his discomfort. A knot of tension rose in her chest. This continual up and down of emotions was like a rough rollercoaster.

He stepped to the side of the path to allow a group of ladies to pass them. Pulling her toward him, she saw concern in his eyes. He asked, "How are you feeling?"

"To be honest, my feet are getting a bit sore now that my shoes are wet. Should we head back to the train?"

"I only purchased a ticket to come here. I have a car to take us to where we want to go next. Are you ready for luncheon?"

"Yes, that sounds wonderful. "They made their way back toward the entrance, where a shiny silver vehicle stood. A man in a black suit exited the car and spoke to them. "Sir. Madam."

He strode over and opened the door for Laura, who turned back to Hugh, her mouth in a huge 'wow.' expression. He smiled back at her.

As he entered the vehicle, Laura leaned across the middle console. "Oh my, Hugh. This is a splurge and a half. What is this type of car called?"

"A Maybach."

"It's beautiful." She ran her hand over the white quilted leather. Sighing, she closed her eyes as the driver's voice carried back to them.

"Where to, sir?"

"Laura, what would you like to do for luncheon?"

"After that rain, a place with soup would be nice. Maybe a salad as well."

Hugh spoke to the driver. Laura relaxed as they sat in companionable silence. The views intrigued Laura and she enjoyed the passing of the city view. Even as her energy drained, she marveled at how she had ended up in London, sitting next to a handsome man. This might happen to young women, but she never dreamed it would happen to her.

She glanced at Hugh, who'd closed his eyes. Long brown lashes dusted his cheeks his profile giving off a strong masculine vibe.

Who are you Hugh, and why are you being so nice to me?

Doubts crowded into her mind. She'd read books about women meeting men like this, but those were in fairytales or sad tales of scammers. Did he think she was a rich American woman? No. He would have seen her attitudes and actions. Like the senior fare on the train. However, that didn't mean anything. Many wealthy people didn't display their wealth. Maybe he just wanted a friend. The problem was, now she wanted more. She'd almost begged Hugh to kiss her when they were stuck in the rain. And then that ... what was it they called it? Oh, yes. Cheeky. She'd given him a cheeky kiss as if to say, go ahead. Kiss me!

He opened his eyes, and she glanced away, embarrassed at being caught staring. "I'm sorry, my dear. I woke early this morning, and the time is catching up with me."

"We don't have to go to lunch. You could drop me back at my place."

"No. One needs to eat. No matter how tired."

"Okay, I just don't want to stop you if you need to go home and take a nap."

"A warm bed with the fire blazing sounds delightful." He took her hand in his. His grip was strong and warm against her hand. Most likely without thinking, he rubbed his thumb up and down her palm.

Whoa there, cowboy. I wanted you to read my mind about a kiss. Not the whole kaboodle.

He continued, "Plus a charming book. And a warm brandy."

Laura cleared her throat. "Yes, that sounds nice. I've spent my days by the fireplace reading while I've been here."

He swiveled in his seat. "Must you return so soon? We are only getting to know one another. I have a friend who owns a home in Hampshire. She requires a pet sitter if you could delay your return."

Laura's heart skipped a beat. *He doesn't want me to leave. He wants me to stay.* "I'm not sure."

"As I had said, I must return to my home soon and if you were there, we could continue our acquaintance."

She nodded. *Acquaintance.* "Why not? You could have your friend contact me, and we could see if we can work something out. I'd like to continue our acquaintance as well." *As well as being in a warm bed by a blazing fire.*

Laura! Get your mind out of the gutter.

She knew deep down there was nothing wrong with wanting love and the physical embrace of a man, even in her bed. It'd been so many years since she'd even thought about intimacy with a man.

Oh, Hugh. It's like you've opened a part of me I thought dead.

The car slowed as they turned onto a street in London. A building came into sight.

"No!" Laura clapped her hands.

"You don't like—"

"Sorry. I meant no in a good way. Like Woo Hoo, yes!"

He chuckled at her words. "You say we Brits have a strange way of talking? Have you visited here yet?"

She shook her head. "No, I've always heard about it and watched it on a television series. I know it looks nothing like back then, but I'm thrilled to see the old architecture. Thank you for bringing me here."

The car pulled up to the curb. Used to stepping out of vehicles by herself, she forced herself to stay put while Hugh's driver opened his door first. Then hers.

She stared up at the building's façade.

Selfridge's.

Chapter Nine

A New Opportunity

"This is delicious." Laura had opted for sea bass after reviewing the menu. Hugh had followed suit with a fish selection of halibut. She speared her fork in the avocado salad with pomegranate dressing.

"I'm glad you like it." Hugh had opted for the same. The nerves from earlier forgotten, they spent the time talking about architecture, things they enjoyed, and any subject that arose. After a delightful lunch at the restaurant on the top floor, Hugh agreed to Laura's request to meander through the various floors, looking at the items on display. Lunch had refreshed them both.

A ding announced that a text had arrived on his phone. Laura glanced over as he pulled it from his jacket, his brows knit together. A frown passed over his face before he regained his composure.

What had the message said? Who sent it? She couldn't pry and he had returned to his placid exterior. A knot in her heart caught her by surprise. She wanted to know what had happened. Even more, she wanted to help if she could.

A display of fragrances caught her eye and she made her way over to them. Various floral and citrusy smells met her as she browsed the various scents.

"Are you going to buy one?"

Laura shook her head. "No. I'm more of a looker than a buyer."

"Well then, you must look to your heart's content."

"I promise I won't take too much more time. I know it's getting late."

As much as Laura had enjoyed the day, she knew her time as Cinderella was coming to a close. She would need to return home to care for the pups for the evening. They'd spent a few hours besides their meal, so she was surprised to see the same car waiting for them outside.

She glanced over at Hugh. Was he wealthy and not telling her? Or was something else at play? Or he wanted to impress her.

Well, if that was his goal, he'd more than done his job today.

She settled into the luxurious seat, wondering how to even address such a thing. You didn't blurt out something like—Hey, are you rich or what? Classical music played softly in the background as they pulled away from the curb.

Yet it also made her wonder why he'd bother to spend time with her if that were the case. Wealthy men, though not all, tended to attract and want young women for arm candy. Unable to decide how to bring it up, she decided to quit trying to overthink the situation. Which would be hard. She sighed with contentment, sat back, and enjoyed the ride back to Queen's Gate.

A soft mist descended as they pulled up to the house. Lights had come on with the earlier fall dusk, and it brought with it a strange mood to their surroundings. After exiting the car, Hugh walked with her up the steps.

Laura faced him, "Thank you so much for today. I loved visiting Hampton Court. You're so knowledgeable and made it come to life. As for Selfridge's, that was another bonus." She hesitated before adding, "As well as keeping me warm and protected during the rainstorm."

"Mm-hmm." He didn't seem his usual self.

"Is everything all right?"

"Yes, well no, not really. Some business issues have come up. I'm afraid I must dash."

"Oh. Sure. Well, goodnight then." She held out her hand. Would this be when he would kiss her?

He took it and bowed over it before saying, "Goodbye, then." Laura watched as the driver glanced at her once more before shutting the door on Hugh.

Goodbye then? Was that it? Had she mistaken a kind gesture as more? It made sense that if you hadn't been around men in decades it would be easy to confuse a friendly action with flirting or more.

She crossed her arms, standing in the hallway. She hated to admit she had wanted it to be more. Even worse, she disliked the feeling. Laura went and checked on the pups who greeted her with tails wagging. They each had a bow clipped to their collars.

"Looks like you two had an enjoyable day at the groomers. Did you enjoy your day at the spa?" Crouching down, she gathered them in her arms. Before she could hold it back, the tears flowed. Great. More tears. I have got to start taking some vitamins or something.

She had been okay being alone. Her life was normal. Meeting Hugh had changed all that. She didn't want to say goodbye. Hanging her coat up, she pulled her phone from her pocket. Glancing at it, she spied a bunch of messages from her daughter, Caroline.

The last one was simple. Call Me!

Already in the middle of the night there, she texted all was well and she'd call in the morning. Whatever issues were going on at home, they could wait. The dogs were back on their beds close to the Aga.

After feeding Sophia and Gregory, she let them out into the garden. Standing nearby she pulled a shawl over her shoulders to thwart off the cold, damp air. She shivered as the dogs made their way inside, locking the door behind her. She made a sandwich with crisps for dinner but the earlier heavy meal meant she picked at the food before putting it away. Pouring herself some wine, she shut off the lights.

"You two ready to go up?"

The pair raised their head but stayed snuggled in their beds.

"I don't blame you. If I had a bed next to that heat source, I'd want to stay there as well. Good night to you." She turned off the overhead lights, leaving on a small lamp and a few nightlights.

Dragging herself upstairs, she set the wine down on a table close to the large clawfoot tub. Drawing a hot bath, she sprinkled in some lavender bath salts, swishing the water with her hand. As the water went into the tub, she strode back into her bedroom, picking up her e-reader.

She needed to complete the book, as the book club would be meeting online in a few days. Since they'd done it so she could join in with them, she wanted to make sure she'd read the book.

Back in the bathroom, she set the reader down next to her wine goblet and a dry towel. Before turning off the water, she added a bit more salts. Laura took her time undressing and lowered herself into the tub. The hot water took a moment before its warmth created a soothing blanket around her skin. She rested her head on the bath pillow, sighing with contentment.

This has been an almost perfect day. His choice of words doesn't mean anything. Hugh was distracted. He'd said so himself.

She didn't want to leave it alone. Though his 'good-bye' wouldn't leave her mind. She rose from the bath, cautious as she stepped out onto the black and white hexagon-tiled floor. Moving to her phone, she texted Hugh.

Just wanted to say again how much I appreciate—

No, not appreciate. She deleted it.—how much I enjoyed today.

She deleted the period.—today with you. Would love to take you to lunch or dinner to thank you. My treat.

Laura stared at the text. Should she say something besides love? Welcome? No, that didn't sound right. Before she could delete the entire communication, she hit send.

There you go. The ball's in his court now.

She stared at the phone, wanting a text to come in. She waited.

And waited.

Nothing.

Now she was getting a chill.

She sat the phone back onto the vanity counter and walked back to the tub where she topped off the bathtub with more hot water. Glancing back at the silent phone, she went over and brought it back to the table next to the tub. Sliding back into the water's warmth, she sipped her chardonnay, and then placed it back on the table.

Sighing that no message came through on her phone, she opened her book and tried to focus on the story. After reading the same sentences over and over, she gave up and put the book down. She picked up the phone, but still no message from Hugh.

Perhaps he's out or in a meeting. He said he had business. Give it a rest, Laura. Plus, he'd been tired. Or having dinner. With another woman?

Jealousy reared its head, and as much as she tried to force it back in its place, it crept into her consciousness. It's not like we're dating or anything. Plus, he lives here. In the UK. She came from the US. It wasn't like things could go any further. Could they?

"Oh, stop it!" Laura yelled. "You're acting like a kid. Just stop it."

Now dressed in silk pj's, she climbed into bed, determined to retain control over her emotions. Her brain agreed. Yet her heart just wouldn't let it go. It wasn't typical for her to be this pent-up with her emotions. Or acting so strangely. She wondered what he was doing. Who he was with. Why had he said goodbye instead of a good night? Her mind refused to rest.

There had been a sudden change come over him after the text. She was doubtful that work could have changed his response to her. What could it have been? A woman.

Refusing to let it go, Laura picked up the phone she'd taken with her to bed. She stomped back into the bathroom and placed it on the charger.

"No more."

She shut the double doors to the bathroom with a bang. Her phone now enclosed in the other room, she piled into the bed. Switching off the light, she punched down the pillow. Closing her eyes, she tried one side and then the other. In frustration, she flipped onto her back, staring at the ceiling.

Why is this happening to me?

Deep down inside, she knew. Laura, a widow, a grandmother, had fallen. And fallen hard for a love that could never be.

The patter of little feet and the sun streaming through the tall windows woke Laura the next morning. She rolled over, looking into their cute faces that appeared to be smiling.

She leaned over the bed, scratching their heads. "Good morning, you two. I gather you're ready for breakfast?" She pulled the matching violet silk robe draped on the bed and stuffed her feet into fuzzy warm slippers. Going into the bathroom, she found the phone, still no message from Hugh. The dogs raced down the stairs.

Plodding down to the kitchen, she started up the kettle to make her French press coffee. Trudging over to the refrigerator, she pulled out the containers with their food inside.

She stole a glance at the clock. She had time to give Caroline a call. First, she wanted to finish making the coffee. It would be early there, but better to catch her before the school runs and work. Opening the side door to the conservatory, she unhooked the door so the dogs could go out to the back garden when they finished breakfast.

Back in the kitchen, the kettle whistled. She poured the water into the pot already prepared with coffee grounds she'd fixed the prior evening. Laura picked up a timer, flipping it over for the coffee.

Once she'd done that, she made her way to the pantry. Finding the scones she'd kept back. She took clotted cream and strawberry jam from the fridge. Cutting the scones in half, she set them on a plate. Glancing at the timer, she moved over and pushed the plunger down on the French press.

All settled, she took the items to a table and chairs in the conservatory, which was filled with greenery. She bit into the scone as she called her daughter.

When the line connected, her daughter's frantic voice came over the line. "Mom. Is everything okay? I tried texting you all day yesterday."

"Yes, dear. Sorry. I was out touring Hampton Court. It's a beautiful—"

"Okay, well, you'll never believe what's going on here."

Laura sipped her coffee. "Do tell."

"What? Are you speaking English to me?"

"No, I was just saying, anyway, doesn't matter. What's going on?"

"Work's been crazy, and now with having to cart the kids around everywhere—"

Laura let the dig at her pass.

"—I haven't had a moment to myself. Then I've volunteered to chair the club's gala this year."

Laura's brow furrowed. "Caroline, don't you already have enough on your plate without taking that on as well?"

"That's why I can't wait for you to get back. Once you're here, I won't have to worry about the school runs, and I can have more time to work on the gala."

"About that—"

"About what? I'm so glad you're coming home soon. I don't know why you couldn't have gone when the kids were out of school."

"Sorry to cause you issues."

Caroline continued, the words not registering, "I hope in the future you'll coordinate with me better before taking off for some indulgent trip because your book club suggested it."

Laura clenched her jaw. "I haven't been away since your father died. And I may be staying longer."

"You can't be serious! I need you here. What am I going to do? You know Frank is worthless with the kids. He's working all the time so it's rare we see him. When he is home, all he does is complain about my work or the kids being involved in too many things—"

Laura set the phone down and put it on speaker. "Maybe he's right."

"You're taking his side now?"

"I'm not taking anyone's side. I'm just making a statement."

"Well, it sure sounds like it."

"Caroline, you can't do everything. It's not possible. I wish I'd have spent more time with you kids and your father instead of all the other things I did."

"What are you talking about? You didn't even work."

The sting of her words hit once again. Caroline always acted as if her mother giving up her career had been easy or that not having one meant she didn't do any worthwhile work. She took a deep breath before answering.

"Hugh has a friend who needs a pet sitter. So I may decide to stay a few more weeks. I'm looking forward to learning more about my ancestors, and this would give me that opportunity."

"Hugh? Who's that?" A silence followed before she continued. "Mom, you're not taking up with someone you don't even know. And at your age!"

"I'm not sure what you mean by 'my age,' but I'm not on death's door, you know. Plus, Hugh's just a friend."

"Sure. Look Mom, I have to run, but please come home. I need you here."

Laura chuckled to herself. Kids never grew out of whining, it seemed. "I'm sure you'll do fine. Now I have to get ready to take the dogs for their walk. Kiss

Frank and the kids for me. Bye." She rang off before Caroline could say anything else.

Staring at the phone, she wondered how many times her daughter had called to find out what she was doing, how she was, or had been excited about anything for her. And that's when it hit her.

She'd been so wrapped in her life as a young woman and wife she'd acted the same with her mother. Her mother may have done the same to her mother. That pull of love and the push for independence had been a constant.

Needing each other but rebelling against it at the same time. Was it any wonder the mother-daughter relationship stayed so fraught with emotional undercurrents?

Laura grabbed her phone and punched in a number. A voice came through the line. "Hello, mom. How are you?"

Chapter Ten

Grand Arrival

In her eighties, Celeste continued to live a full life. Between pickleball, lunch, and dinners out with friends, and involvement with her church and a local nonprofit, she stayed busy. Laura admired her mother for it.

Growing up, her mother's life, as many mothers do, revolved around her children. Between activities, she often could be found cleaning or helping a neighbor.

Is this why Laura had adopted the same attitude or lifestyle?

When Laura first told her mom about the book club ladies, her mother asked for Laura's impressions of the ladies. She'd been happy about 'that feisty one' who'd recommended Laura consider pet sitting so she could visit London. Celeste had encouraged Laura to go when she got cold feet at the prospect of traveling alone.

Her mother had been her biggest cheerleader, egging her on. "What's that phrase your ladies all say? Take a chance! You know you're not getting any younger. I wish I could go back and not be so afraid all the time. When you get to my age, you're like, what's the worst that can happen? Because just getting up from the bed and not falling could be an adventure."

Laura laughed. "Mom, you're one of the fittest women I know. You put me to shame!"

"It's the inside that's what's important and has all the fun. Well, mostly." She giggled.

"Mom, I can't believe you said that."

"What, you don't think I know about sex? How do you think you got here?"

Laura shifted. "You know what I mean. All kids know it. We just don't want to think about our parents doing it."

"Pshaw. Stop being such a prude, Laura Jane."

She exhaled. "I'm not a prude. Let's change the subject."

"Okay. I wish I could have gone with you. But next week is a bridge tournament and I've already committed to it. Now you have fun!"

"I just feel bad about leaving Caroline to deal with the kids and everything else."

"Good grief. The woman's in her forties. You've always coddled that kid. Quit treating her like a child, and she'll quit acting like one. Plus, that good-for-nothing husband of hers can chip in and help."

"I don't know. Something seems off about him. I've noticed Caroline seldom speaks about him anymore.

Only to say he's swamped at work and traveling a lot for business."

Her mom whistled. "Oohwee. Sounds like he's got some side action."

"Mom, why do you say that?"

"It's all the signs. Trust me, I know."

Laura jolted. "Wait, what? How would you know?"

"Let's just say there was a time early in our marriage where one or both of us could have strayed. Luckily, we both realized how much we loved one another and nipped it in the bud. Midlife crises are no joke."

Laura brushed her hair back off her face. "I hope you're wrong."

"Me too. Now tell me more about what's been happening with you. How's the trip going? Is it everything you thought it would be?"

And more. Laura thought to herself.

"Yes, I've enjoyed walking with the dogs, and you wouldn't believe the home I'm staying in. If you can even call it a house. It's one of those places you'd see in a British drama about upstairs and downstairs.

Technically it's a townhouse, but it still has a wrought iron black railing and a gate for where the servants used to get inside the house. Now it's used for deliveries and taking the dogs out, and there's also another kitchen down there for when they have events. It's like nothing I've ever experienced."

"Lucky girl. Now what else? The others can wait for me to show up. It's normal for me to be the early one, anyway."

"Well, I've learned some more about our ancestry. And yesterday I went to Selfridge's and ate dinner at their restaurant."

"How nice. Did you go by yourself or with someone?"

Laura debated how to respond.

"Ooh, that silence means it was a man. Spill the beans. Or I guess since it's in England, spill the tea."

"He's just a friend. I met him while I was walking the dogs. And he happened to be at the pub. It was crowded, so he offered to share his table." She didn't elaborate on him paying for the meal or walking her home and kissing her hand.

"Sounds nice. Are you seeing him again?"

"I'm not sure. Yesterday we went out to Hampton Court, as that's where our ancestors lived."

"Fun. You'll have to tell me more about what you found out. But not right now. Anything else before I have to hang up?"

"I may have another pet sit I could do. It would be easy enough to change my ticket. I made sure I included that in case I had to rush home. Caroline wants me home, but—"

"Absolutely not! You stay and enjoy this time away. This is the first time you've gone anywhere since John died. It's time to live a little. Mama's orders!"

Laura laughed. "Okay. It's not for sure. I'll find out in the next day or two."

"Great. Keep me posted. Now I have to go, or I'll get an earful from Norma. Love you."

"Love you too, mom."

The line went dead.

The conversation concluded. Yet a worrying thought niggled in Laura's mind. She'd thought Caroline's moods could be attributed to starting to go through the change. Or was there something more? Something that she didn't want to talk about. All marriages had their difficulties, but could this be something else entirely?

She sat her phone on the table when she heard the front doorbell chime. Laura made her way to it, opening the door to a man holding a box. "Sign here, please."

Laura signed her name before taking the box from the man. He tipped his hat and raced back down the stairs to a green van. Laura watched as he merged into traffic before closing the door and locking it behind her. She took the heavy box into the kitchen. It didn't have a name on it, so she untied the ribbon around the box.

Inside was a crystal vase nestled in bubble wrap, though her breath caught at the sight of a large batch of pink and cream peonies. As she picked them up, a card fell out onto the table.

A reminder of our delightful day yesterday. Hugh

He'd remembered. Before the rains had forced them to flee inside, they'd been able to walk by the beautiful floral hedges including pink peonies. Laura had remarked that they were her favorite flower.

Joy bubbled in her chest, and she beamed. While the flowers were beautiful, him listening and remembering what she'd said was an even greater gift. His thoughtfulness delighted Laura. She buried her face in the flowers, enjoying their fresh floral scent.

Laura set the flowers back down before taking the vase out. Filling it with water, she felt a renewed sense that last night had not been a final goodbye. Using a pair of scissors, she clipped the protective papers and the lower stems to place the peonies in the water.

Since she already had the flowers from the other day, she took these new arrivals upstairs. Setting the beautiful pink and cream display on a table in front of the window, she admired them again. This way she could enjoy them the moment she woke up and when she went to sleep.

Returning downstairs, she texted him a thank you. Again, no return text came through.

"Come on. Let's get our walk done." She leashed the dogs who were hopping around her feet with excitement, Grabbing a wool scarf from the hook near the door, they went out the back stairs to the garden.

The crisp weather had Laura pull on her gloves as the trio walked through the park. Breathing in the earthy smells of the grass and trees, her mind calmed.

She'd arrived back at the house when her phone rang. An unknown number. Laura didn't answer unidentified numbers, but as this was a UK number, she answered.

An older woman's voice came across the line. "Hullo. Is this Mrs. Rollins?"

Laura knew better than to answer yes on a call so scammers could use her voice. It didn't matter as the woman continued, "This is Dorothea Meriweather."

The name sounded familiar. Then she realized it was the person Hugh had noted might need a pet sitter. "Yes, hello. You can call me Laura."

"Laura, I hope that I am not intruding at an inconvenient time."

"Not at all."

She put the phone on speaker so she could unleash the dogs. They sat at her feet, waiting while she rummaged in a nearby jar for puppy treats.

"Perfect. Hugh informed us you are a pet sitter, and we will be going away for a fortnight to our house in Provence."

Of course, you are. Who doesn't have a house in the south of France?

Dorothea continued, "Might you be able to watch our animals whilst we are away?"

The pups took their treats and headed off to their cozy beds by the Aga. Laura put the kettle on to make tea before picking the phone back up, and taking it off speaker. "What are the dates? I have to finish this sit which ends in two days, and then there would be additional time if I had to travel. Where are you located?"

"Surrey. Colton Hall. We have one dog, Fergus, and two cats. Sweetie and Pippa."

Dorothea talked about the requirements for Fergus and a little about the cats.

"Seems straightforward enough," Laura replied.

"Brilliant."

As the pot started whistling, Laura moved the boiling water from the bob. "Is there a train that comes to you or a bus? I don't have a car."

"You can take the train down to Farnham, and then we can pick you up in the car and take you to the hall."

"Um, I appreciate the opportunity, but without a car, how will I get to the grocery store?"

"It will all be sorted for you. We have a man who can take you into the village for anything you may require. The village is a short walk. You can go to the pub, and he can pick you up when required."

Oh, how the other half lives. Of course, you have someone to drive you around.

Dorothea continued. "Matthias is our foreman and takes care of the stables."

"Oh, you have horses too?" Laura had always been drawn to horses.

"Yes. Do you ride? If so, I can have him fit you out on a pony while you're here."

"I've ridden horses, but it's been a while."

The woman continued, "Hugh could ride with you. He is expected down at his house during the week. He also has horses."

Laura's heart skipped a beat. Hugh would be nearby. How bad could it be?

"That sounds wonderful. Would you like me to send some references?"

"Smashing. We'll see you then. You can call this number to let us know the train details and arrival time. I look forward to meeting you."

"You too. Thanks." Laura ended the call.

Why hadn't she done this before? She needed to give Betsy a big hug when she got home.

She poured water over the tea to steep. Once ready, she added a bit of milk to it. Unlike many American kitchens, this one boasted a loveseat and chair as well as a small table. Picking up her tea, she set it down on the piecrust table next to the chair. The Chinese porcelain lamp with its colorful birds on it cast a glow in the room.

Laura sat in a big, cushy chair to read her book, and sipped at her Darjeeling tea. She'd added a couple of sugar cubes to it. The milky sweetness on her tongue soothed her. before long her eyes were drooping. She gave in to the kitchen's warmth and allowed herself the luxury of a nap.

Chapter Eleven

Special Request

The next few days dragged by. Being away from Hugh wasn't easy. Since her thoughts were of him when she woke, during the day, and before she fell asleep, she tried to keep herself occupied but the struggle often defeated her efforts.

When the couple returned, the trio went to the pub. They wanted to express their gratitude for taking good care of Sophia and Gregory. They dined on fried fish and chips, though Laura had decided mushy peas weren't for her. Plus a beefy brown gravy was a different condiment than the tartar sauce or ketchup she normally used.

Returning to the house, the couple bid her goodnight as Laura would be leaving early the following morning.

The first rays of dawn had broken the sky with pink painting the clouds when Laura made her way downstairs. Amber insisted on getting up to take Laura to the train station. Piling her carry-on into the Range Rover's back, they set off for the short journey.

Hugging goodbye with statements to stay connected, Laura pulled her case behind her into the station.

Even though it was early, it was busy with people hurrying to catch their trains for work or travel. She'd have loved to sit and watch people pass by but there weren't any benches. She made her way over to peer at the screen display to find the train's platform number.

After taking the train during her stay she'd learned to look for other stops along the way to her destination. Finding the right platform, she walked with others up the stairs and across to go down the second set of steps toward the waiting train.

She found her number in the car, settling into the cushy seat. An older gentleman across from her nodded his head before returning to his book. Paying for seating in first class had been worth it. Once they'd left the station Laura took tea and sipped at it as the view morphed from city to countryside. Before long, they were pulling into Farnham station.

Pulling her bag from the luggage rack, she adjusted her purse on her shoulder. Stepping off the train, she held onto the cool grab bar, ever wary of 'minding the gap' she set her bag down. On the platform, she moved out of the way of people rushing so she could pull the handle up on her carry-on.

For whatever reason, travel gave her a joy she hadn't realized she'd been missing. Even in a country so similar, its differences were a delight to see and experience. Laura joined the throng of people leaving the station as she made her way toward the car park. Laura was walking toward the exit when she saw a handsome older couple headed toward her.

The attractive, petite woman with silver hair spoke. "Excuse me, are you Mrs. Rollins?"

"Yes." Laura set her bag upright to free her hand. She held it out and Dorothea took it before releasing it. She spoke to the gentleman beside her who bore a full head of gray hair and a trimmed beard. "Darling, will you take the bag from Laura?"

He nodded before speaking to Laura. "I'm Clive Meriweather." He did a slight bow of his head.

"Nice to meet you."

"We're on the second floor of the car park. Shall we?"

Laura replied with a favorable response as she followed along to the car.

"I've taken the liberty of purchasing some items for you until you can go to the store. Should you require anything else sooner, please do let us know. We have all of today so that we can pop over to the shoppes for whatever you may need."

"That's wonderful. Thank you again for coming to pick me up."

"I wouldn't dream of you finding your way to the house without us driving you. Here we are. "Dorothea pointed to a silver Mercedes.

Clive opened the front door for Dorothea before beckoning to the back door. He opened it and Laura settled in behind the front passenger seat. As they drove out of town, Laura appreciated the bucolic scenery during their drive. She'd seen pictures, but seeing the sheep grazing on the hills in person continued to delight her.

Passing through a village, a small enclave of homes appeared. As they drove into the gates, Laura glimpsed a three-story home.

Dorothea waved to the beautiful Georgian home. "Colton Hall."

Tall eight-to-ten-foot windows with mullioned casements were on the main two floors with smaller six-foot windows on the top floor. The red brick was old, and the front had a vine covering the downstairs front and around the windows. The house also had an abundance of fireplaces, at least six on the main house's roof with another four on what appeared to be a later wing extension.

Laura refrained from a "Wow." She couldn't hide the irrepressible smile or stop the fluttering of her heart. She'd pinch herself if she didn't know for sure she was awake.

They pulled up to the front door, and Laura did her best not to gawk at the gorgeous facade. First staying in the London townhouse, and now this. She couldn't have wished for anything better.

Exiting the car, she waited as Clive pulled her luggage from the vehicle's trunk.

"My dear, you must be tired from your journey. Would you like to see your room first or shall I show you around?"

"I'm fine if you'd like to show me around. You have a beautiful home."

Dorothea smiled. "Thank you, my dear. It's been in Clive's family for hundreds of years. It's Grade II listed with the National Heritage List for England. Clive's family took care of updates over the years, so we didn't have to deal with anything upon our move here."

Laura cocked her head. "I don't mean to be rude, but am I wrong? I detect a different accent."

"No. You're correct. I was born in the United States, but my father and mother came over after the war. Of course, they had American accents, and over time, I picked up more of a British accent."

"I know that there are as many English accents as there are American ones, but I did notice it a bit in yours."

Dorothea said, "Let's begin with the ground-floor rooms, and then we can continue to the first-floor rooms." She led the way through tall mahogany doors. Sliding them apart, the view of the fireplace caused Laura to gasp.

"I'm sorry to be so transparent. I'm simply in love with architecture, and this room is stunning."

Dorothea smiled at her response.

"Thank you. It's refreshing to hear someone express what they think. I had the same reaction the first time I arrived here." She strode into the room and pointed out the doors leading outside. "These lead out to the veranda. Now let's go over across the hall to the dining room."

The stunning dining room mirrored the formal reception room's beauty. Fit for entertainment, the room held an extended polished cherry table with fourteen chairs. Another massive fireplace stood as the focal point along a full wall. Patterned wallpaper did its duty to incorporate access doors on either side of the fireplace. After touring the ground floor, they took the marble stairs up to the first floor.

"You are welcome to spend your time anywhere you choose but these are the family rooms. If you'll please follow me, I'll show you the snug."

"I'm sorry, what?"

Dorothea laughed. "It's what we call a small, comfortable room."

"Oh, like snug as a bug—"

"Yes. Rooms that are more for the family and smaller in comparison to the rooms downstairs." Laura followed Dorothea as she walked down a hallway. This was an adjoining wing Laura had seen on their arrival. She opened a door and allowed Laura to pass into the room.

Windows brought in light, giving a nice glow to the room. A smaller fireplace took center stage along one wall. A warm fire crackled and glowed in the hearth. Shelves filled with books lined two walls and Chesterfield sofas and chairs dotted the room.

"I can see why you refer to this as the snug. It's so inviting." Laura said.

"Thank you, my dear. Now let me show you to your room. Then you can settle in, and I'll show you the back stairs that will take you into the kitchen. And you can meet Fergus."

"Sounds perfect."

Coming to the hallway's end, Dorothea opened a door with the back stairs.

"These will take you down to the kitchen." She shut the door and continued to the hallway's end. Opening the door, she motioned for Laura to enter. "Please let us know if you require anything else for your stay. Cook will make you whatever you'd like for meals, and I'll introduce you when you come down to the kitchen. For now, I'll leave you to it."

She closed the door behind her, leaving Laura standing in a room that was as big as her entire garden home. On one wall, a four-poster bed held pride of place across from another fireplace. It had been lit as well, a wonderful welcome to the home.

A loveseat and two high-back chairs were positioned around the fireplace. The tables were adjacent with beautiful porcelain lamps that brought a soft glow to the room. Laura walked over to the tall windows which turned out to be French doors.

She pulled them open and strolled onto a balcony with balustrades that overlooked a side garden. Along with topiaries, a fountain bubbled in the middle of a gravel walk.

Someone pinch me. I can't believe I get to stay here.

Back inside the bedroom suite, she spied a door hidden in the panelwork. Pressing her hand against it, it opened into a bright and light bathroom, more modern in approach than her bedroom. Her suitcase sat on a bench.

Laura's brow furrowed. These people have more money than I'll ever see. Why don't they just hire a pet sitter? Plus do they still call people by their titles like cook or whatever?

Laura wandered around for a bit before opening up her suitcase and hanging everything up in the large armoire and nearby dresser. After a quick shower, she put on a casual dress, before taking the back stairs down to the kitchen.

Inside the warm room, Dorothea sat chatting with a young man. A golden retriever jumped up from his bed, prancing over to her, wagging his tail.

"Let me guess. You must be Master Fergus." Laura scratched under his ears. He gave the typical grin of his breed.

"Quite. He thinks he's master of this house to be sure."

The young man came over, his hand extended. "Hullo. I'm Cook Norby. General all-around help."

Laura stifled a chuckle. "Nice to meet you, Cook. Laura."

"Cook keeps us set with meals during the day and some basic running of the place. He's training as a chef, though we would hate for him to leave us. So if you like trying new dishes, you'll enjoy your stay here."

He followed Dorothea in saying, "I dish up something for lunch for the staff and then do some practice dishes for evenings twice a week. If you have any preferences, let me know, and I'll do my best to supply them."

"That's very kind. I'm sure that whatever you create will be delightful."

Dorothea added, "It's nice to have the lunch done and a few nights' dinners too. The older we've gotten, the less we like to bother. When I found out that Cook was learning, I offered our kitchen to him. I hated to see this place not receive much use."

"I can understand that. It's one of the nicest kitchens I've ever seen."

Dorothea smiled. "We agree but it's too much for us. And as we eat lighter at night or head out for dinner this suits all around." She indicated an area apart from the kitchen. A warm fire lit up the small woodstove. "This is where we usually have breakfast. There is another larger room that we use for lunch and dinner that is across the hallway. I can show you later."

"I'm sure this will be fine as long as I won't be in anyone's way here."

"Certainly not. You're now the lady of the manor in my absence so feel free to choose where you would like to sup."

"Thank you. Oh, and what about the kitties?"

"They do their own thing. You'll see them occasionally but not much you'll need to do on your part. They do like to sit in your lap if you have got a mind for that. However, they won't bother you if you don't like it."

"Sounds nice."

"Now I'm sorry to be the bearer of unwelcome news on your arrival, but Clive is feeling poorly and has gone up to our room. He begs your forgiveness. If you don't mind my dear, I may excuse myself from luncheon with you and ensure that all is well with him."

"Sorry to hear that. I hope he feels better soon. Don't feel you need to entertain me. I'm perfectly content reading my book. Oh also, I do have an online meeting with my book club. Could I get the Wi-Fi information from you?"

"Cook, can you please help Laura with that?"

He nodded, whisking something in a bowl. "Yes."

After Dorothea excused herself, Laura sat at the table with a pot of Earl Grey tea. She sipped at it while she gazed outside at a potager garden. Tension from her earlier travels released and her shoulders relaxed. Her thoughts were interrupted when Cook set a bowl of steaming white soup before her.

She tasted the hot potato leek soup. Oh, wow. This is delicious. Hungry from the morning muffin she'd grabbed on the train, she emptied the bowl. As she took a last spoonful, she wondered if it would be bad manners to ask for seconds. She didn't have to think more about it. He came over and removed the soup bowl.

Oh well. If she needed something else, she had some granola bars in her bag upstairs.

"Here you are." He placed a dish before her that held a pastry including chicken and mushrooms. A side salad accompanied it as well.

Taking a bite, flavors mingled with tarragon filled her mouth. "Wow. This is really good."

He beamed. "Thank you. It's a new recipe I'm trying out."

"It's divine." She took another bite of the flaky crust, moist chicken flavored with a hint of sage, and smoky mushrooms. Finishing her meal, she rose from the table, taking her plate with her. Cook was stirring something on the stove.

"Not to worry, love. I'll take care of that. Now would you like some treacle tart?"

Laura patted her stomach. "That was delicious, Cook. I'm stuffed right now."

He nodded. "I can bring some up to the snug later. I'll need to check the fire anyway."

Laura handed him her plate. "Do you think it's okay for me to check out the gardens?"

"Sure. If you go through the hedge there it will take you to a beautiful outlook over the village. You can continue on and then follow the path back to your right and it will bring you to the side door."

"Wonderful. Thank you." Laura meandered through the gardens. Along the path, roses and other flowers brought contentment through their beauty. She came to the overlook. The village looked like something from a picture postcard. Cottages and houses dotted the landscape while white specks dotted the hills. More used to seeing cows, the sheep supplied a bucolic scene.

Who knew something so simple as a country-side view could make her so happy? She took a deep breath, exhaling again as happiness filled her. Though she needed someone to share it with her.

Laura's thoughts turned to Hugh. For the first time in years, she'd enjoyed a man's company. He was not only handsome. He was attentive, charming, and all the things that made a great companion. A great partner. Yet something had occurred when they were on their outing. A barrier Hugh had erected from her.

Her thoughts drifted to what Dorothea had said. Laura stifled a giggle. Lady of the Manor. Lady Laura. That has a nice ring to it. Imagine what my kids would say.

Her thoughts reminded her of her last conversation with Caroline. She should try to call her back again.

Returning to the house, she stepped inside the mudroom when Cook poked his head out of the kitchen.

"Message for you. They took it up to your room. The fire has been poked in the snug, and the treacle is waiting."

"Thank you."

A message? From whom?

Chapter Twelve

Fish Out of Water

Laura took the back stairs to her room. Opening the door, she looked around. She glanced over to a floral vase filled with greenery and flowers from the garden. An envelope sat on a silver tray. She opened the cream-colored envelope and withdrew the cardstock inside.

It was an invitation for dinner in three days at Hugh's home.

A postscript had been added stating that he would send his driver with the car.

Dinner at Haradon Hall.

If that house was anything like Dorothea's, then it would be something else. Not a dinner where she could show up in her regular clothing. Looks like she owed Sylvie an apology. That blue dress would be perfect.

After returning from their walk, Laura spent the rest of her day reading. Clive felt better, so they drove over to the village where they dined in a pub named the White Hart. After an enjoyable evening, they bid her good night.

The following morning, Laura rose early to wish them goodbye. They were heading up to London and then taking the Eurostar over to Paris, France. After a few days there visiting friends, they'd make their way south.

At the car, Dorothea took Laura's hand. "It was delightful to meet you. I hope you enjoy your time here."

"That's very thoughtful. Thank you so much." They did the prerequisite air kisses, and Laura waved as they drove down the gravel drive.

Back inside, she grabbed up a Macintosh and wellies before putting Fergus on his lead. The morning held the promise of a perfect fall day. As they walked, the fallen leaves crunching beneath their feet broke the silence that surrounded them. Trees, now shed of their canopies, were lone sentinels along their path.

"Fergus, I bet this is beautiful in spring with all the bluebells dotting the ground." He wagged his tail as Laura crouched down to scratch behind his ears. She stroked his soft, silky fur as he bathed in her attention. Standing, she added the leash to his neck so they could head off. The weather

They walked for miles, and Fergus was able to run for a bit without the leash. She snorted with laughter at his antics, running in circles and stomping. He would dash over to a pile of leaves, twirl around in it, and then dash to another area.

Knowing that he had more energy than she had stamina, she called Fergus to come. He rushed over, his tongue hanging out, his tail thumping on the ground. "You're such a good boy. We're going to have such fun, you, and I."

They returned to the house as fog rolled in, bringing with it the promise of rain showers. Fergus went to his bed, twirling around before plopping down on it, a grin on his face as he closed his eyes. Laura shucked her boots and jacket before taking a moment to watch Fergus.

If someone wants a picture of happiness, it's right here. When had she stopped enjoying the simple things of life?

Cook had taken off for the afternoon, so she had the house to herself. Having only a cup of coffee before their walk, her stomach rumbled.

Laura pulled out some egg salad and made a sandwich. She munched on salt and vinegar crisps. Looking in the fridge she spied some of the treacle tart. The tart lemon filling and buttery crust hit the spot.

Satisfied with her meal, she fiddled with the invitation she'd brought into the kitchen with her.

Her mind raced at the possibilities as well as possible gaffs. She bit her lip, as irrational worries grew. Shaking her head at her constant dwelling on the what-ifs, she stopped. Have I always overthought things?

Worried about things instead of enjoying the moment?

She sat back against her chair. Thinking back over the time she'd been in England, she realized how she'd fought with emotions and facts.

Once she'd cleaned up her meal, she spied the cats wrapped around each other on the window seat. "Hello, you two." She stroked their backs before leaving them to check their automatic feeders and bubbling water station.

Not ready to head upstairs, Laura took the opportunity to view the home's décor at a more leisurely pace. Wood paneling and other embellishments had been cared for over hundreds of years. The home's history was almost palpable. Laura meandered around the ground floor. The lone sound in the cavernous space, the prominent grandfather clock ticking the seconds away.

Laura stared at the clock. Time ticking away reminding her of the need to embrace the simple moments in life. How quickly she moved from a child to a vibrant young woman and now to a woman in the wonderful fall of her life. Fall. A time to drop things that no longer served her. To enjoy more of what she wanted. If she only knew what the things were she should give up and which to gather.

Using the front stairs, she walked to the snug. Opening the door, she saw Cook had set the wood for a fire and a tea service sat nearby with a cozy over the teapot. A glass-domed plate displayed flaky scones, while a pot of cold lemon curd, and one with clotted cream sat next to it.

She smiled at the thoughtfulness. He had to have done this before he took the Meriweathers up to London.

Striking a match, she lit the fire.

I'm beyond spoiled. I won't want to go back.

Full still from her earlier meal, she decided to save the scones for later. Plus, it was almost time for her to jump on the computer for her book club meeting.

Laura strode to the nearby desk and opened her computer, readying the camera for their discussion. She clicked through to the link. Everyone had agreed they would meet early as this month's selection had been Laura's.

Angela had made it challenging as they each picked a genre, but then another note held additional criteria. For Laura, it had been a book set in the UK with a woman's name. Laura had selected *Rebecca*.

The ladies' arrival in the chat room focused her mind.

Shirley came on first, punctual as usual. They were saying hello when Betsy arrived. Claire followed and they had to tell her to unmute herself. Francis came on, and then Sylvie arrived, apologizing for being late because of her busy schedule. Busy or not, Sylvie tended to be late for everything. Betsy even chided her for continually needing to make an entrance.

Laura addressed them, "Should we wait for Angela?"

Betsy replied, "No, she said she was sorry but couldn't join us. To go on without her."

"Oh, okay. Well, first thank you all for doing this. I didn't expect to be staying longer."

"It's fine," Shirley replied while Francis nodded in agreement.

"Tell us all about your trip," Claire interjected.

Laura took a breath. "Well, you wouldn't believe the places I've been staying."

Betsy interjected, "I don't know if that background is anything to go by. But if so, wowzer!"

Laura remembered the fire crackling in the hearth behind her, with the large windows draped in heavy curtains on either side. Though the sofa obscured much of it, there was a glimpse from the desk where she sat.

Claire chimed in. "Is that a library? I adore a roomful of books."

"I guess you could call it that. They call it the snug."

"Oh, that's a nice name," Francis replied.

"Yes, the rooms on the ground floor are huge. They use them more for entertaining which I think they do quite a bit."

"How fun. Have you met anyone?" Sylvie chimed in.

"What do you mean by that?"

"Your face is flushed. You have! Spill the beans," She continued.

Laura cleared her throat. "His name is Hugh. We'd had dinner, and he escorted me to Hampton Court to see it. He found out my ancestor may have lived there."

"That's exciting," Francis remarked.

Laura nodded. "Yes. He's the one who got me in touch with the Meriweathers. I don't understand why they need a pet sitter. They could pay for the service or get Cook to watch Fergus. Though I guess it's a bit like my first sit. They need someone in the evenings and overnight."

"They have a cook they call cook?"

Laura laughed, "Well yes, and no. Cook is his real name, but he is their cook too."

"What do you have planned while you're there?"

"Hugh's invited me to a dinner party at his house. And yes, Sylvie, it's a good thing I bought that blue dress. I owe you one."

"A woman always needs to be prepared for any occasion. That's my motto." Sylvie pulled her wavy blond hair back into a messy bun.

Claire interrupted. "So you met him in London or there?"

"He was in London for some business, I think. He lives in Hampshire."

Betsy said, "Sounds fancy."

"His house is called Haradon Hall. If it's anything like the one I'm staying in, then it's fancy. Plus, he's sending his driver to pick me up for the dinner."

"His driver? Did you snag a prince or something?" Betsy laughed.

"No, but I do feel a bit like a princess. Even Dorothea said I'm the lady of the manor while she's gone. It makes me feel, I don't know. Special. Which is silly at my age."

"It shouldn't. You're already special to us, dear Laura. Enjoy being pampered," Claire added.

"I guess. It's a bit like a dream I don't want to wake up from."

Sylvie moved closer to her computer. "So, this Hugh? Anything serious there?"

"No. I don't think so."

"I think you're holding back. You like him!"

What's not to like? He's handsome, charming, and thoughtful. Instead, she replied, "He's a nice man."

"Mm-hmm." Sylvie countered.

The ladies all laughed.

"Okay, this isn't supposed to be talking about my trip. It's supposed to be about the book. What do you all think about it? Claire, why don't you start us off?"

"I've read this book before, but I enjoyed reading it again. There's so much there but especially why the first Mrs. DeWinter was still in the picture. Then you have the conflict between an American wife and the formal English housekeeper."

"Have you noticed anything like that with your being American?" Shirley inquired.

"Only once. There was a bit of a misunderstanding. Entirely my fault. I thought Hugh had called me a name." She proceeded to tell the group about the incident with the dogs.

Betsy howled with laughter. "Oh my gosh. I'd totally forgotten about that. That's so hilarious. I can see me doing something like that but not you Laura. You're so proper."

"Well, I wasn't so proper that day. I was fuming. Later, I realized that I'd misunderstood what he said. Then I felt really foolish."

"It happens to the best of us. No matter. It sounds like you left enough of an impression for him to ask you to dinner," Claire added.

"That was another coincidence. He rescued me at a pub. Some men had been in their pints for a bit, and he came to my aid. We ended up eating dinner together."

"That sounds wonderful. He could be a keeper," Francis said.

"Except that he lives here, and I live in the States. My daughter's already been upset that I'm staying longer."

"Kids can manage their own lives. We raised them. We don't need to continue to be at their beck and call," Francis replied.

Sylvie interrupted. "Well, you have to tell us about this dinner. Do you know who else is invited?"

"No. I guess I'll find out when I arrive."

"Well, you have to let us know. What if it's just you and him?" Sylvie winked.

A shiver went up Laura's spine. She composed herself before replying, "I don't think so. He sent me a printed invitation, so I think it's a gathering."

Betsy swiveled her chair. "Just a bit of advice, Laura. Don't let them Brits walk all over you."

Laura balked, "What do you mean?"

"I'm glad you're taking those chances we talked about. Just don't let any posh people look down their noses at you. That's all I'm saying."

"I think you've been watching too many shows. Everyone has been genuinely nice."

Betsy shrugged, "Just watching out for you."

"And I appreciate it. In fact, I appreciate all of you. I have to be honest. I wasn't sure about participating in the book club. I didn't know any of you. And well, our first meeting was, um, interesting."

Betsy threw back her head, her laughter pouring forth. "You mean me and Sylvie getting into it. We're over that now. Right, Sil?"

Sylvie rolled her eyes. "Sure. Anyway, I know meeting you ladies has made a difference in my life."

Laura nodded, wondering if everyone else had the same thoughts. Sylvie seemed to have cut back on her drinking, so that was a good sign. Though she knew she still wasn't being completely forthright with them.

"Listen, we've barely talked about the book. I feel like I've been a terrible hostess for our first book club meeting."

Claire said, "What are these clubs for anyway? Women and words. We can share about the book. I've been looking forward to learning more about you all."

Shirley nodded. "I guess I should confess too. I was going to drop out. Our connection through the weeks has made me appreciate the need for women in my life."

"I'm so glad, Shirley. I appreciate your insights as well," Claire responded.

"Okay, well should we at least rate the book?" Laura asked the group.

They all chimed in with some holding up fingers.

"Looks like a winner," Betsy said.

"Well, good. I guess we should sign off. It's getting late here, and I'm sure you all have busy schedules today."

They all shared their goodbyes, each leaving the meeting. Laura sat in front of a blank screen. She looked at a message that had come through. It was from Francis.

"Make sure you let us know how the dinner goes."

Sylvie had posted for her to send a picture in her dress, while Betsy had ended with her current chorus of 'take a chance.'

Take a chance. But at what? Laura knew the answer. At love.

Chapter Thirteen

Shocking Announcement

Laura devoted her time to getting ready for the dinner. First a nice long soak in the bath with music playing in the background. Putting on her fluffy robe, she spent time doing her nails. When they were dry, she used a hot roller to set curls into her hair.

She messed with it for a bit before landing on an updo. It would be manageable for her to achieve on her own. Plus, adding curls would give her hair more body. On the plus side, if any slipped from the pins, the style would still look nice.

Her hair set in curls, she spent the most time on makeup application. Lastly, she stepped into the dress along with simple short kitten heels. Because she'd brought minimal jewelry with her, she put in the pearl studs to finish her look.

Twirling from side to side in front of the mirror, she admired herself. "Not bad for an old lady, don't you agree?"

The woman in the mirror smiled and nodded.

She let out a long breath to release the tension. A simple dinner.

If only she could convince the butterflies in her stomach who were having none of it. They flitted about busily.

And it wasn't just a dinner. It was a dinner with Hugh's friends. If his male friend had been any indication, most wouldn't be keen on her and her American thoughts and ways. Especially if history had anything to say about American women causing issues.

Sitting in the bergère chair of checked pastel moiré fabric, Laura took five deep breaths. Clasping her hands together, she forced herself to be calm. Everyone gets butterflies when they go into an unfamiliar environment. Or at least she did. This would be her night to shine, and nothing and no one was going to stop her.

She rose and smoothed down her dress, thankful the velour material flowed and didn't show wrinkles.

It wasn't cold, but there was enough of a chill that she would need a cloak for the evening. When she'd contacted Dorothea to tell her how Fergus was doing, she'd asked about a shop where she could purchase a wrap.

In response, Dorothea asked Laura to send her a picture of her dress, saying that she'd manage it for her. Worried Dorothea would purchase something way out of Laura's budget, she tried to decline politely. The woman must have realized Laura's quandary, as she said she wanted to gift her the wrap as a thank you for watching Fergus.

A few hours later, a package arrived. A long cape with slits for her arms looked as if it were made for her dress. Included were cream gloves, something Laura hadn't even thought about, along with a small clutch purse in a rosy blush color. Perfect with her shoes.

Dorothea had gone above and beyond. Phoning Dorothea to thank her, she offered to repay the woman for the expensive items. However, Dorothea rejected her offer.

Laura picked up the velvety cloak and fastened it around her neck. There came a knock on her door. It was Cook.

She opened the door.

He grinned. "I hope you don't mind my saying so, but you look lovely."

"No, us old gals will take all the compliments we can get."

He opened his mouth to reply but must have thought better of it. Instead, he smiled at her. "The driver's downstairs. May I escort you down?"

"That'd be wonderful. Thanks." She grabbed her bag before shutting her room door behind her.

As they made their way to the front door, another knot of butterflies arrived.

This can't be real. I must be in a very lucid dream. Please don't wake up yet.

"I'm sorry. What did you say?"

Oh no, had she said it out loud?

"Nothing. Just me muttering under my breath."

"Right-O. I'll leave the front door open. I'm down to the Horned Toad with some mates, so I'll lock up everything when I get home."

"Thanks, Cook. For everything."

He did a bow with his head before opening the front door. Laura descended the exterior stairs to the waiting car. She spoke to the driver. "Hello again. How are you?"

"Well, ma'am. May I?" He opened the door, and she found herself once again in the Maybach. Blue lighting along the sides gave a soft glow to the interior.

She settled in as he closed the door and went to the driver's seat on the vehicle's right side.

Laura thought it would be nice to drive the wonderful back lanes, but she still didn't feel comfortable enough driving from a different steering position. While Betsy had advised keeping the road's middle line off your shoulder, lots of back roads didn't have any lines. And with large hedgerows along the sides, seeing ahead also made maneuvering difficult. Yes, there were lay-bys, as they were called, but she still didn't know the rule of who uses it. If she came back, she'd need to learn more about it. Having a driver was the next best thing.

Sitting back against the warmed seats, her nerves settled. She'd eaten a late lunch, so maybe that had caused some of her stomach upset. Cocktails at eight with dinner afterward meant that a couple of cups of coffee had been on the earlier menu. She didn't want her energy to crash at the party. That must be why those earlier jitters were so noticeable.

The driver's voice came to her. "Would you care for some music, Madam?"

"Yes, that would be nice. Um, I wonder what some older classics from England would be?"

"Are you familiar with Paul Williams?"

"Oh, yes. I recall his *Life Goes On* album from my youth. That would be nice, thank you."

Soon the sounds of "Save A Dream For Me" surrounded her with a soothing melody. It was without a doubt a night of dreams. Who could ever have imagined that Laura would end up like this? She wanted to enjoy it as long as she could and stop being afraid to break whatever spell was in the air.

The lights faded as they made their way deeper into the countryside. The night sky shone with stars sparkling against a black sky. Soon a sprinkling of lights appeared. The car slowed as they pulled up to the large iron gates. Lights dotted the drive as they drove under the canopy of trees that blotted out the night sky.

This must be beautiful in the daytime, she thought.

The car took a turn, and as they did, Laura caught her first look at the house.

Like Colton Hall, Haradon House bore a Georgian home facade. Laura thought back to her earlier college learning and recalled the style of Neo-Palladian. Symmetry across the front face supplied guests with a sense of awe and splendor. Colton Hall could have been an apartment in comparison to the house before her. It boasted a magnificent set of tall, highly polished double doors. The windows on the main and first floors lit from within causing the house's appearance to glow against the darkness.

She gulped. *This is Hugh's home?*

Tears sprung to her eyes, and her stomach knotted. All this time. Hugh hadn't said a word. Or caused her to feel small. A wave of gratitude swept over her. He'd not demeaned her about the train ride or paying for their tickets. He'd treated her with respect. Yet, there was no doubt that they were from two different worlds. No, make that planets.

Her hands twisted in her lap. *I'm out of my depth here. What if I make a fool of myself?*

She fought the temptation to ask the driver to take her back to Colton Hall. She pondered if she could feign a migraine. Her mind raced with some way to bow out gracefully.

Tires crunched on the gravel as the car came to a stop by the front door. The driver exited before she spoke.

She let out a deeper breath as he opened the door. "Um, I'm not feeling too well. If I should have to leave, how can I contact you?"

He bent closer, his voice quiet. "You can do it, ma'am."

She swallowed hard, breathing out. Placing her hand on his, she replied, "It's that obvious?"

He didn't respond but tipped his cap. "Should you need me, all you need to do is let Thomas, the butler, know."

"Thank you." She picked up her dress's hem to mount the steps to the door which had opened on their arrival. Inside, a man in a tuxedo welcomed her, while a woman in a simple black dress offered to take her cloak.

After removing her gloves, she handed them to the woman, who smiled and moved toward a door concealed in the paneling. She handed the cloak and gloves to a younger woman and took her place back at the door.

The man Laura figured was the butler spoke. "If you'll follow me, madam."

Oh no. Now that she thought of it, should she have left her gloves on? Too late now. Laura fought hard not to stare at everything she passed. The ceiling in the foyer boasted a magnificent chandelier, and the marble floors were covered with stunning Persian rugs.

They made it to the entrance where a suited man opened the doors. Inside, a fire blazed in the fireplace. Women in beautiful gowns and men in evening attire were scattered around the room.

"Mrs. Rollins." The man announced.

While a few looked in her direction, most stole a glance while continuing their conversations. Laura was glad of that, as she already felt on display. She entered the room, where Hugh came over to greet her.

Oh, thank heavens. Laura felt her heart and mood lift at seeing him.

He bent close to her and she took in his masculine scent. "Laura, love, let me introduce you around."

Hugh led her around the room, introducing her to the various individuals and couples. While polite, Laura sensed a chill toward her. She'd heard that Brits often looked down on Americans, but while that may not have been true, class distinctions seemed at play here.

After making the rounds, a man came up to her, asking if she would like a drink. "Um, yes. I'll have whatever Hugh is having."

The man's eyebrows lifted a fraction. Oh no, had she already made her first faux pas? What should she have said?

Laura smiled and pretended to listen to the conversation until the man arrived back with her drink. She took a sip, but the drink didn't hit right. Oh, no. Gin. Of course, gin and tonic would be the drink of choice here. She'd always thought gin tasted like diesel fuel.

"It doesn't suit you?" a male voice inquired. She found it was the man from the first day when she'd met Hugh in the park.

Oh no. He must have seen the face she made. "Oh, hello again. To be honest, no. I'm not a fan of gin."

Conversation stopped. Heads turned.

"What would work for your American taste?" His voice had taken on a tone of condemnation.

Hugh had been chatting nearby and overheard. He came to her aid. "Would a vodka martini suit?"

"Yes, please." She wanted to add 'for my American taste' but bit back the retort.

After she received her drink, Hugh stayed close until dinner was announced. As they walked to the dining hall, Hugh strode to the head of the table. Laura waited until she was escorted toward the opposite end of the table. She looked back to see Hugh whispering to a beautiful blonde woman on his right. He didn't appear happy, but the woman touched his arm as if to settle him.

Servers came in, and the dinner began. Laura perched on the edge of her seat, grasping her hands under the table to steady her nerves. She was no stranger to attending nice dinners, but this was taking her to a place she'd never been before. She allowed those on either side to carry the conversation, turning it back on to them at every opportunity.

Laura breathed a sigh of relief when it was announced coffee would be served in the lounge.

The men rose but lagged behind in conversation while the women left the room. With the many courses, Laura needed to find the ladies' room. She inquired with one lady who had her follow her to a room where women already congregated.

Voices flowed as she waited her turn. More than one complimented her on the dress she wore. One even gave her an expressed approval on her hairstyle. She relaxed a bit as the women's voices rose with their chatter.

This would be okay after all. They didn't seem to look down on her as an American. She'd probably imagined it.

From her place, Laura watched the women as they reapplied lipstick or primped in front of the mirror. A lady passed by her, and it was her turn. Closing the door behind her, she took a moment to breathe. Her emotions fraught after the dinner, she wished there were a window she could climb through. Unable to hide in the toilet any longer, she stepped out to allow another woman to enter.

After washing her hands, Laura made her way to the outer room where the mirrors were. Setting her purse down, she took out her lipstick. She applied it to her top lip when the blonde woman she'd seen sitting next to Hugh joined her at the mirror.

"My dear, that dress color is divine on you."

"Thank you." Laura moved the lipstick over her bottom lip.

"I dare say we weren't properly introduced earlier. I wasn't able to speak to you at all before dinner."

Laura finished swiping the stick along her lower lip. The woman handed her a tissue, which she used to blot her lips. "Thank you. I'm Laura." She put the cap back on her lipstick, clutching it in her left hand.

Instead of responding in kind, the woman remarked, "The American staying over at Colton, correct?"

"Yes, I'm watching Fergus while they're away on holiday."

The slender woman scrunched up her nose. "Not a fan of the beasts myself."

"I love animals," Laura replied.

The woman put her comb back into her clutch. "Do you ride horses?"

"It's been a long time, but I love to ride horses."

"You must come and ride with us this weekend. I'm sorry, please tell me your name again."

"Laura." She held out her hand to the woman who looked down at it.

"Oh yes, I remember now."

She held out her hand. "Georgina. I'm Hugh's wife."

Chapter Fourteen

Chaos and Calamity

The room spun.

Laura's lipstick clattered to the floor as it fell from her hand. She clutched at the counter. Her legs refused to hold her up. Her breath grew shallow as she struggled to remain standing.

No. It can't be. Wife? He'd never mentioned it—then again, why would he? Sweat broke out on her forehead. Her stomach roiled.

Please no. Don't get sick.

"Oh, my dear. You don't look well. Here, have a seat." Georgina led Laura to a nearby mahogany chair.

Laura could feel the flush creep up her neck. "I haven't been feeling well. I may leave and go home." She found a vacant chair and collapsed into it. Some women paused and looked at her but said nothing before exiting.

Georgina came over to Laura. "Oh, that would be such a disappointment to Hugh. But if needs must. Should I call the car?"

"That'd be wonderful. And if you don't mind making excuses for me." Laura placed her hand on her stomach, though the real ache was in a much different spot. She fought against her rising emotion.

"Indeed." Georgina picked up the handset of a vintage phone that sat on a nearby table. She dialed a number.

"Send the car around. Yes, the American lady is not feeling well." Georgina paused, listening to the person on the other end. "No, that's not necessary. I'll speak to Lord Haradon concerning her departure." She set the handset back in the antique telephone's cradle.

"Now then, can I get you a wet washcloth or something to drink?"

Laura shook her head. "No, I'm fine. I just need to get my cloak."

"Let me walk with you. I do hope you'll still consider going riding with us this weekend."

Laura cleared her throat. "Thank you, but I didn't bring the right riding attire, and I'll be leaving soon."

"Are you? Back to America, then?"

"Yes. I have to get back to my daughter and grandkids."

Georgina took Laura's wrap from the young woman who brought the coat. "Of course, my dear. Here, let me help you with this."

Laura turned as Georgina placed the cloak on her shoulders. "Thank you for your help. Will you please tell Hugh—I mean, Lord Haradon, that I had to leave."

"With pleasure."

The front door opened, and Laura constrained herself not to rush down the steps to the car. She forced a smile on her face as she waved at Georgina. The slim woman stood with the hall's light at her back, a stunning figure in the night.

Inside the car, her body shook with emotion. She glanced up to see that a partition had been raised between her and the driver. Thank heavens. She didn't know if she could continue the charade of being okay any longer. It was then and only then she allowed the breaking of her heart to turn into deep, heart-wrenching sobs.

Why am I so stupid? I never should have come here. She pulled a tissue from a box in the console, dabbing at her eyes.

This was no dream. This was a nightmare. And she wanted to wake up.

What had she been thinking?

That she'd come to the UK, find a handsome, attentive, wealthy man, and what? It was all fine and good to daydream about such things. Reality hitting you full force was another matter. Had he seen her the way she'd seen him or as a doddering old woman from America who needed help? And what about Georgina? She hadn't even used her name when she called for the car. It had been 'that American woman.'

Like good riddance to bad rubbish. Is that the way Hugh felt about her, too?

No, she couldn't see him doing that. He had treated her with the utmost respect. Or had it all been a game to him?

Maybe goaded on by his friend who hated Americans. 'Hey, I'll wager you. A thousand pounds, you can't fool that woman into thinking you love her.' Or had it been all about the money? She hadn't cared about Hugh other than as a man. The wealth, the title, and the mansion meant nothing.

Only him.

A man who'd stolen her heart.

That was the crux of it. She believed when their eyes met that he felt the same as she did. His touch had sent shivers down her spine and tingles in her hand when he kissed it. Had he felt nothing at all?

When she spied the lights of Colton Hall relief flowed through her. Stepping from the car, she stuck her hand out to the driver.

"Thank you for driving me and everything. I'd offer you a tip, but that may be perceived as bad form. Sorry, I'm not up on all of the British customs. If I gave you this as a token of everything you've done for me, would that be okay?" She held up a twenty-pound note to him.

He hesitated before accepting it and putting it in his pocket. "Ma'am, it's a pleasure to drive you." He tipped his hat, refusing to say anything else.

"Well, then, good night. Or I guess I should say good morning."

Ah, how apropos. After midnight turning back into a middle-class woman. But this was no Cinderella story. More like Grimm. She never should have gone to dinner.

He waited until she had made her way to the front door and opened it. She turned and waved back at the driver.

Geez. Another thing I probably shouldn't do.

He drove off as she stepped inside the foyer and closed the heavy door behind her. Inside the house, she leaned against it. The wood cold on her back.

So what if it wasn't done? She didn't care.

The grandfather clock chimed the hour. Three in the morning. When was the last time she'd been out that long? At least not since her college days. She started as she heard a noise.

It was Cook. "Did you have a wonderful evening at the manor house?"

She didn't want to say much, afraid she'd break down in tears again. Instead, she smiled and nodded. She said goodnight to Cook before rushing up the stairs. Inside her room, she slammed the door behind her. Leaning against it for a moment, she took deep, cleansing breaths. Tears stained her cheeks. When she'd calmed, she pulled off the velvet cloak and gloves.

Laura shucked out of her shoes, kicking them across the room, and as she did, her hurt turned to anger. Its ugly tentacles grew.

Who was he to play with her like she was a toy? Did he think that he could treat her like dirt because he thought she was a poor, daft American? Well, no more. That Laura was done with him. He'd never faced the Laura who could give as good as she got.

She shimmied from her dress and into her pj's and robe when she sat down at the desk. She'd left the computer open. She glanced at it to see messages from the Boomer Babes, as they liked to call themselves. One popped up. It was from Sylvie. It read, Call us as soon as you're up. We're dying to know how it went.

Oh, that's right. It was in the evening at home. She opened the program but kept her camera off.

"Hi, Sylvie."

"Hold on. I know the other girls wanted to jump on."

Before she had a chance to stop her, the other ladies joined the call. She took the time to wipe her face and compose herself. Then turned her camera on.

"Tell us about it. We can live vicariously through you. Was there dancing?" Francis asked.

"Francis, I think that's the only thing you think about sometimes," Sylvie chided.

"It's not. I just love it, that's all."

"Ladies, let Laura speak." Claire's teacher's voice took command of the situation, causing the others to stop in mid-sentence.

Laura looked at the women whom she had met a few months ago. She felt like she'd known them forever. Sylvie, who had been so polished and put together when they'd first met but held secrets of her own. Francis and Shirley were coming out of their shells more and more. Claire, who had appeared to be above everyone else when they'd first met. Once you got past her noble façade from years in an Ivy League university setting she revealed herself to be a genuinely pleasant woman. And Betsy, who reminded Laura of a golden retriever who blurted out whatever was on her mind without thinking or holding back. Each woman a salve to her spirit.

Each so unique in personality, but all caring and wonderful women. They were kindred spirits and much needed in her life.

That's when she lost it.

"Oh, honey, please don't cry," Shirley cried as the others chimed in.

"Do we need to come over there and give him 'what-for'?" Betsy interjected.

Laura grabbed a tissue from the container on the desk. Taking in a deep breath, she told the women about Dorothea and her gifts. Hearing that, Sylvie had her model for the cloak for them.

The woman couldn't contain her excitement. "That's stunning. When you come back, I want to borrow it."

Laura nodded before draping the garment over a nearby chair. She pulled another tissue dotting her eyes.

Claire spoke, "You take your time, my dear. We're here when you're ready."

"His driver came to pick me up—"

"Ooh, hoity toity." Betsy said, before being shushed by Claire.

"Turns out Haradon House is a mansion. Well, that's not even the right word. It's a palace, almost. And he's not just Hugh. He's Lord Haradon."

"Wow. I can see it now. Lady Laura Haradon."

Laura sighed. "No. Turns out there's already a Lady Haradon."

"What! Why that no-good—" Betsy rose off her seat.

"Are you sure?" Shirley interjected.

"Oh yes, I'm quite sure. She's a stunning, slender blonde. And quite a bit younger, to boot. Her name is Georgina."

"Who has a name like that? I don't like her already." Betsy ignored Claire's admonitions to be quiet.

"I guess his wife. And while most were nice, he has this friend who hates Americans. He wouldn't say anything outright. No, it was more like little digs. Like me not liking gin."

"Ugh, me either. It's nasty," Betsy chimed in.

"Agreed. I'd much rather have something made with vodka—or well, now I'd prefer something else." Sylvie twisted a lock of hair with her finger.

"A gin and tonic is quite good, on occasion," Francis said.

Claire cut through with her powerful voice. "Ladies, we're getting off track. It wasn't about the drink, but the person. Now Laura, don't let those uncouth individuals ruin your evening. There had to be some highlights?"

Leave it to Claire to bring the conversation around to something good. Laura nodded. "First, of course, I felt like a princess. I have you to thank for that, Sylvie. I got complimented on my dress by some of the other women there. And the house, well, it's something out of this world. It's like you stepped back in time to something out of Austen's work—"

"Hey, it's our book club selection come to life. Manderley!" Betsy interjected.

"Yes, that's correct. At least as big as that. One of the most beautiful houses I've ever seen. And what's funny, it didn't feel showy. It felt as if the house were giving you a hug when you came in the door. It sounds weird—"

"No, it doesn't. I had the same feeling when I visited Rome and stood in the square. I honestly think that environments, places, and even houses have emotional components like people. That's why you can visit someplace and feel a desire to leave right away," Claire replied.

"I never thought of it like that, but you're right. I've been to people's homes where I've felt welcomed in and comfortable and others where I wanted to leave quickly."

"So what about this, Hugh? Or Lord Haradon? Do you plan on seeing him again?" Sylvie asked.

Laura shook her head. "No. I'm guessing he was simply being polite to a stranger." She didn't share her earlier thoughts.

Betsy crossed her arms. "I don't know. Sounds like he was leading you on. You should tell him to 'sod off.' Isn't that what they say over there? And what does that mean, anyway? Get off my grass?"

Shirley and Francis laughed. That started a trickle effect, and soon the entire group was roaring. They'd collect themselves and then someone would say, "Get off my grass!" And they were off again. Tears streamed from their eyes as they tried to compose themselves, but to no avail.

"Stop looking at me!" Betsy cried out.

"You stop looking at me," Francis responded.

"Get off my grass!" Sylvie said, and they all broke down again.

When the laughter had run its course, Laura looked at each of the women.

"Ladies, I want to say something."
The group quieted.

"I'm almost ashamed to admit this, but well, here goes. I almost quit the book club right after we met. The first meeting was, shall we all agree, interesting."

Sylvie and Betsy groaned at remembering their first encounter.

Shirley nodded her head. "That's one way to put it."

"Anyway, I just want to say I'm so grateful I met you. You aren't just my friends. You're sisters I never knew I needed. I don't know what I would have done without you. You've been here to encourage me to take a chance."

She stopped to wipe away a tear. "Not everything we try in life works out the way we thought it would. But that shouldn't stop us from taking those chances. I've loved coming to the UK and seeing things I've only seen online. And meeting such wonderful people."

Francis sniffed, caught up in Laura's emotional display. "Even Hugh?"

Laura took a moment before responding. "Even Hugh. He's made me see that I can love after John.

I can feel attractive and desirable to men. Even if it wasn't to be with him, he's opened the door for me. I'm in a much better frame of mind about even thinking about a relationship with a man again. And this never would have happened if not for you all."

Betsy winked, "Well, we have the kindred spirit piece covered."

Everyone broke out in laughter again. When they'd composed themselves, Shirley asked, "What will you do now?"

"I have a week left. I'll take care of Fergus, and then it will be back to shuffling grandkids around."

Betsy interjected. "You don't have to go back to the 'same ol,' same ol.' This is just the beginning."

"Yes, but for now, it's just the ending. And as it's three in the morning over here, it's time for bed."

"Okay, hugs!" The group went around saying goodbye until the screen went black. Laura smiled. She'd neglected friendship as a busy mom, then a grandmother. Never again. Her friends had been the perfect salve for her bruised heart.

She climbed into bed and relaxed into a peaceful sleep.

She woke to birds chirping on the trees outside her window. She stretched and pulled her fluffy robe from the bed. Half-asleep she put on her slippers, before making her way down the stairs. A sharp knocking at the front door woke her fully.

Who would be here now? Were they expecting a package? She tightened her robe around her and went to the entrance.

Opening the door, she gasped.

"Mom!"

Movement caught her eye. Not only had her mom arrived but so had her daughter. Celeste moved aside as Caroline rushed into Laura's arms, sobbing.

Ah, the nightmare continues.

Chapter Fifteen

Disappearance

Laura waited for her daughter to compose herself. After ushering the pair inside, they talked over one another making it hard to understand anything. "Stop. Let's go sit down and have something to drink."

Is it too early for a shot of something strong?

She led her mother and daughter into the kitchen, who oohed and aahed behind her at the house. Once in the kitchen, Laura set the kettle on the hob for tea.

After pulling out cups and saucers, she faced the pair. Laura leaned against the counter.

"Okay, who's going to tell me what's going on here?"

Her daughter let out a combination sob and squeal. "Frank has left me!"

Knowing she was going to have a tough time getting any more information from Caroline in her state, Laura stuck her hand up for her mother to continue.

"Caroline called me up and said Frank had given her an ultimatum. He was fed up and wanted out of the marriage."

"Okay, but I still don't understand why you two are here. In England."

Her daughter wiped her eyes. She took a few quick, shallow breaths. "He told me to talk to you and that you're the only one who has any sense in this family."

Laura pursed her lips to hide her smile. Well, at least someone respected her opinions. Even if it wasn't her daughter.

Laura rubbed her face and wiped her eyes to wake up. She yawned. "You know I'll be back in a week. Why are you here?"

Celeste interjected, "He said that he'd keep the kids and for Caroline to get away and to do some serious thinking about their marriage. So when she told me, I said why not come over here and surprise you?"

Laura crossed her arms. "Gee, thanks."

"Well, you know kids always need their moms in times like this." Celeste rose from her chair when the kettle whistled.

"I'll take care of it, mom. You just sit there. So that explains why Caroline came here, but what about you?"

Laura took the kettle from her mother and poured the water into the teapot to steep.

"I'm no young chicken. If she was coming over to England, I figured I'd join her. I've heard you discovered some things about our ancestry and thought it'd be a fun trip."

"Mom, you're in your eighties. Don't you think that was a bad idea?"

She pushed her shoulders back and struck as much of a pose as a scarcely five-foot woman could strike. "I may be old, but I'm not dead. If you can travel alone in your sixties, I can travel here with my granddaughter."

"I just turned sixty." Laura fumed as the latch on the back door opened. Cook strode in, and as he saw the three at the table, he stopped. "Well, hullo. Did we have a party on the calendar and I didn't receive the invite?"

"Cook, this is my mother and my daughter. They decided to surprise me."

He came over and grasped Celeste's hands. "Delightful." Then turned to Caroline. "Charmed."

He set his hands on his hips. "All right then. Who's up for a full English breakfast?"

"Me!" Celeste spoke before Caroline shrugged.

"Laura? You know you want some beans on toast too." He grinned, knowing Laura wasn't a huge fan of the protein-heavy breakfast.

"Fine. Please let me help you and then I need to find a place for them to stay. Do you know of a bed-and-breakfast or hotel nearby?"

His brow furrowed. "Let me check on that. I need to grab some gear from the Morris, but I'll be back in a moment."

"Okay." Laura used a strainer over the cups as she tipped the teapot to add the brewed tea.

She gazed at the two women who she loved so much as they jabbered together. This might turn out fine. They could do some sightseeing together.

Cook reentered the kitchen, holding a box in his hands. "That's all sorted."

"What is?"

"I spoke with Dorothea. She said that you are to have your mother and daughter stay here. She wouldn't hear of you finding a hotel."

"I can't do that."

"Why ever not?" Her mother chimed in.

"Because this isn't my home. I'm here as a sitter. Not as a guest. I mean I am, but—"

A chime let them know someone had arrived at the front door. Laura threw her hands in the air. "Is this Grand Central this morning? I'll see who it is." Laura left the kitchen and headed to the front door.

Opening it, she came face to face with Hugh.

"Oh! It's you!" It was at that moment she remembered she was still wearing her pajamas and robe. She'd forgotten to run a brush through her hair before coming down earlier. She tucked the wayward strands behind her ears. Embarrassment flaming her cheeks.

He stood silent, waiting for her to invite him inside.

"Oh, sorry. Come in."

She closed the door behind him, her heart pounding.

She wanted to yell at him, 'Why didn't you tell me you were married?'

She also wanted to collapse into his arms and never leave. Fighting so much emotion within, she decided to take a stoic path.

"To what do I owe the pleasure of your company?" If he wanted to play games, she would show him a thing or two.

"I wanted to inquire after your health. I didn't find out until earlier that you had been ill last night. I'd just been told you needed to leave. I hope it was not something to do with the meal."

She wanted to say it was something to do with your wife. Instead, she replied, "No." Laura turned to hear footsteps behind her. Oh great, her mother and daughter had followed her out to the foyer.

Her mother took a step forward. "And who is this dashing gentleman?"

He took her hand and bowed over it. "Hugh."

Celeste dithered like a schoolgirl over his attentions.

He spoke to Caroline. "You must be Laura's daughter. I've heard about you and how proud your mother is of your achievements."

Caroline caught Laura's eye, a flush on her face. "Um, nice to meet you."

Cook came out to the foyer. "Lord Haradon, we're having a fry-up. Would you care to join us?"

Standing behind Hugh, Laura gave an agitated shake of her head. It was too late though. She tried to avoid the wide-eyed stares of her mom and daughter at hearing his name spoken.

"I don't wish to intrude."

Celeste put on fake airs. "You wouldn't be intruding."

Laura's eyes widened at her mother, frustrated at her acting and asking him to join them.

He turned to Laura, who forced a fake smile on her face.

"If that's acceptable."

"Sure. Why not? Now, if you all don't mind, I'm going up to change."

"Oh, run along, darling. We'll keep Lord Haradon company." Her mother beamed at him as he escorted her toward the kitchen.

Just great. She flew up the stairs as the group moved back into the kitchen.

Could this day get any worse?

✦

Breakfast turned out fine, though Laura pushed around much of the food on her plate. She wanted to speak to Hugh alone. Why couldn't he stop being his charming self with them? If they only knew what a cad he really was.

With their meal over, he rose to leave. "Ladies, it was a pleasure to meet you both."

"It was nice to meet you, too." Celeste put out her hand for him to take.

Caroline nodded her agreement, though her mind was elsewhere.

After rising from her chair, Laura gave them the 'You stay here' look behind his back. They walked into the foyer, and she opened the door.

"Well, thank you for stopping by to check in on me."

He stepped closer, and her heart flipped. She stepped back.

"Laura, I feel I have offended you. Please let me know what I've done so that I can address it."

"There's nothing to address. Thank you for the invitation to dinner last night. Since I'll be leaving soon, this is goodbye." She held out her hand, ignoring the hurt look on his face.

"Laura." He came forward, placing his warm, strong hands on her upper arms.

"Please don't." She moved away from him, biting her lip to stop herself from crying.

He dropped his hands and made his way out of the open front door. Turning back, he glanced at her, hurt on his face.

No, she wouldn't feel sorry for him. She slammed the door.

Resting her back against the cool wood, she closed her eyes, fighting against the tears. When she opened them, her mother and daughter were standing in the hall.

Celeste's face bore the look of a brewing storm. "What did he do?"

Laura strode over and the three embraced.

"Well, this is a fine mess. Let's sit down and you can tell us all about it." They went into the formal living room as Laura didn't want Cook to overhear their conversation.

After Laura shared their first meeting in the park, the dinner, and then his taking her to Hampton Court, both her mom and daughter were in awe.

"It's like something from one of those romance movies." Celeste twittered with glee.

Caroline nodded. "I mean a real Lord. Few can say they've met one unless you run in those circles."

"You should see Haradon House. It makes this one look tiny in comparison." Laura slid back in her chair.

Celeste huffed. "Then what's the problem? He seems a nice enough fella. Good looking too."

"There's one big problem." Laura's jaw tightened.

"Oh Mom, is he one of those guys with the title and big house but needs money from an American?"

Laura laughed, "Caroline, this isn't the nineteenth century. Plus, I'm sure it's clear to him I'm not made of money."

"Maybe not. He may think that's just the way Americans are. I hope you weren't fooled into giving him any money. I hear about scammers all the time preying on older women." Caroline picked at a piece of lint on her sweater.

Laura bristled. "Caroline, I'm not stupid. I haven't given him any money."

She rose from her seat, pacing back and forth. "I'm sorry. I've been out of sorts the last few days over it. Anyway, he's paid for all our outings. He's a wonderful, kind, caring man."

"Then what's the problem?" Celeste asked.

"His wife."

"What?" they chimed.

Laura sighed and fiddled with her hands in her lap. "Last night I went to a dinner party. While there, I met a beautiful blonde. Georgina. She told me she's his wife."

"Oh no. Honey, I'm so sorry. Do I need to go over there and give him a good talking-to? Or I should give him a slap for hurting my kid." Her mother waved her hand back and forth before acting like a ninja.

Her antics broke the tension. "Sure, mom. You can kick him in the knee."

"Fine, but I'll do whatever you need." She let out an enormous yawn. "Maybe after I take a nap. Traveling and the time change is creeping up on me."

"Let me find out from Cook what rooms you will be staying in. Just stay in here, and I'll find out."

Laura found Cook cleaning up the breakfast dishes. "I'm sorry. I should have helped you instead of running off like that."

His brows furrowed. "All sorted. Is everything all right?"

She shrugged. "I'm sure it will work out. Now, what room should I put my mom and daughter in?"

"I've already taken the liberty of putting their bags upstairs in their rooms. Let me show you where they are."

They got Celeste and Caroline from the living room, and Cook led the way upstairs. He opened some doors to two more bedroom suites. Celeste and Caroline oohed and aahed over the beautiful landscape seen from their windows.

"Thanks, Cook." Once he'd left, Laura hugged her mom. "Sorry about earlier. I didn't get much sleep last night, and I'm cranky. I'm glad you came. Now, take as long as you want. I need to walk Fergus, but I'll be back later."

She left Celeste opening her suitcase and walked over to the adjoining room. Laura stuck her head in the open door. "Caroline, are you okay?"

"Yes. I think I'll indulge in that large bath I saw in the bathroom."

"Ooh, that sounds nice. Having a hot bath sounds good right now. And it may help with any jet lag."

Caroline rushed over and hugged Laura. "Mom, it sounds like we both have man problems. I'm sorry about what's happened. I like him. He seems like he's a nice man, and handsome and rich to boot. Plus, he couldn't keep his eyes off you."

Laura wanted to bask in that thought but replied, "Well, he better place them back on his wife."

"I bet you could take her in a fistfight." She winked.

Laura laughed. "Sure. I'll remember that if it comes to a duel. Now, if you need anything, I'll be back in a while. Or you can always find me too. My room is just down that hallway and there's also a snug on the right. Anyway, I'll see you two later." Laura held onto the door as she stepped back out into the hallway.

Caroline asked, "Is there something else, Mom?"

Laura nodded. "Caroline, you let me know when you're ready to talk about what's been going on with Frank. My shoulder is here for you."

"I will. I feel a bit shell-shocked right now. I don't even know why I'm here. Or what I'm doing. Mom, I—" Tears sprung to her eyes.

"It's okay. We can chat later. Now you go enjoy that hot bath." She hugged Caroline.

She went downstairs to head out for her walk. That's when she realized Fergus was missing.

Chapter Sixteen

Confession Time

"Fergus! Where are you, boy?"

Cook had left so there was no way to ask him. In his haste, he hadn't noticed Fergus behind him. She went through into the back mudroom, but Fergus wasn't there.

Cook would have had to have seen Fergus here, but maybe the dog had slipped around him without him noticing. Laura went outside, calling for the dog, but to no avail.

Her feet crunched on the gravel as she jogged to the back gardens, but still no cheerful dog running up to meet her. Laura continued calling his name as she strode toward the house.

No sign of Fergus.

The cats swished their tails as she went over to them. They'd been easy to care for while she'd been there.

If only Fergus had been as easy. She racked her brain as to where Fergus might have gone.

She'd been told he enjoyed hanging out in the warm kitchen and would go to the other areas if others were around. Maybe he had come into the formal living room when they were chatting and fallen asleep.

Then he couldn't get out when he woke, since she'd closed the heavy sliding doors behind her. With renewed pep in her step, she made her way across the cavernous foyer.

With a cheery voice, she pulled the doors open to the reception room. Laura called out to him. Again, no Fergus. Walking around the room, she explored various nooks and crannies filled with warm light where he may have lain. No luck.

There was one other place to look before she panicked. She hurried to the snug upstairs. Had he gone upstairs looking for her or the others? He'd been her shadow most days. Going back through the kitchen, she took the back stairs Fergus took with her in the evening.

Reaching the upper hall, she called his name again. A door opened. It was her mother.

"What's going on?" Her mother wiped her face.

"Oh Mom, I'm so sorry. I didn't mean to wake you."

"You didn't. After hearing what Caroline decided to do, I thought a hot bath would relax these old stiff bones. Now what's with calling for Fergus?"

"I went downstairs to take him for his walk, and he's missing. I've looked outside, in the main rooms, and now here. I can't find him anywhere."

The dam broke. Huge sobs came from her, and she stepped into her mother's room and sat down on the couch. "Oh, Mama."

Celeste came over and sat down beside Laura.

"Honey, we'll find Fergus. But this isn't about him, is it?"

Laura sniffed. "No, I suppose not."

A hand came into view, holding a bunch of tissues. Caroline had joined them.

Laura took the offered tissues. "Oh, no. I'm sorry. Did I interrupt you too?"

Caroline shook her head. "No. I was on the phone with the kids. I haven't even had a chance to grab that bath yet."

Laura nodded before blowing her nose. "I think it's just a bunch of things all at once."

"And the fact that you love Hugh." Her mother patted her leg.

Laura shifted, "Why do you say that?"

"Because you can't hide it. It's as plain on your face as if someone had written it on your forehead. I've seen it just a few times over my life. It was definitely on yours." She stopped for a moment before continuing, "And his."

"But he's married. And that's—um, really, he had that look on his face?"

Her mother nodded.

"Well, it doesn't matter. As I said, he's off the market. And I will never be accused of being a home-wrecker. And I'm way too old to be someone's mistress."

"I think there has to be more to it." Caroline walked over to the window and looked out. "I feel it in my bones."

Laura replied, "Oh well, if you feel it in your bones, then."

"Mom, don't be patronizing." She faced her, arms crossed. It reminded Laura of her as a child when she'd try to get her way by taking that stance.

Laura wiped her nose with the tissue. "Have you ever listened to yourself? You, of all people, shouldn't be giving me love advice when your marriage is in a shambles."

Celeste shifted and looked at Laura. "And yours was perfect?"

"Well, no. But John and I stuck it out."

"Did you?"

"What are you talking about? Yes, we did."

"I guess you don't recall all the times you came over with the babies complaining about John, his neglect of you, how you were going to leave him."

"Really, gran?" Caroline came over and sat in a chair opposite them.

"Oh, yes. Am I right, Laura?"

"Well, maybe when I was younger, but I don't recall ever saying I was going to leave."

"You did. Marriage is the hardest and the loveliest thing you can experience in life. It's work. It's frustrating. Conversely, it's joy and love. And when the lust is tamped down from life's stresses, that's when you find that those vows were important. There is a sicker, poorer, or all the other things that make up a life, that's when true love shines."

She took a breath and patted Laura's hand. "Now, this shows that your heart is open to love again. And that's a good thing. Yes, it may hurt, and yes, it may not turn out the way you wanted. You already said you wouldn't change meeting Hugh. So are you already throwing in the towel?"

"No. I guess not." Laura wadded up the tissue and threw it in the trash by the desk.

Caroline moved away from the window. "Mom, what did you want?"

Laura sniffed, "What do you mean?"

"Well, did you expect him to propose to you? To ride off in a golden carriage to his palace? What?"

"I don't know. I'm confused. He could have originally thought I had more money and could help him. Or perhaps he realized I'm just ... me."

"But that's not what matters. Is it?"

"No. I just want to be with him. That makes me sound like a teenager who's got a crush on the quarterback who's way out of her league."

"No, it doesn't." Celeste rubbed Laura's back.

"Mom, he's not in *your* league," Caroline said.

Laura rose and went over to her daughter. "Thank you for saying that. "They embraced and Laura pushed the hair back from her daughter's eyes. "What about you? What do you want?"

Her daughter broke down in tears, crying on her mother's shoulder.

"If you two don't stop it, we'll all be crying," Celeste said.

Laura handed Caroline some tissues and directed her to a loveseat. "Mom, I've been so busy getting ahead at work and taking care of the kids' needs—"

"That you've lost yourself."

"Yes." She nodded. "Frank and I live separate lives. In some ways, I don't blame him for giving me the ultimatum. He wants to slow down more, and I feel I'm just going to gain some freedom in a few years. I don't know what I want, and I don't know what to do. When Gran said to come here, I jumped on it. I didn't know what else to do."

"Well, I figured if all three of us smart women can't figure everything out, what good are we?"

Laura said, "Well, the first thing we need to do before conquering the world's problems is find out where Fergus has gone. He's my responsibility, and I'd feel horrible if something happened to him."

"I'm sure he's fine," Caroline added.

She looked at her daughter who'd turned to face the window.

Celeste rose. "Agreed. He's got to be somewhere in this big house."

Laura nodded. "I'm sure he's dreaming of chasing rabbits right now. We just need to figure out where that might be."

"Okay, we'll start the search. Together. For now, can I get a cup of coffee? That tea didn't do it for me," Celeste said.

"Sure. You two get some clothes and shoes on for going outdoors, and I'll make the coffee. I can also call Cook and see if he knows anything."

Caroline started. "Oh, I wouldn't bother him. He told me he's taking the train and won't be able to answer his phone."

Laura cocked her head. "What aren't you telling me?"

"Nothing—"

"I've known you since you were a baby, and I also know when you're not telling the whole story. What were you and Cook talking about when I came downstairs from getting dressed?"

"Wait, I remember now. I did see Fergus follow Cook outside. Cook said that he'd left something in his car," Celeste chimed in.

The two looked at Caroline, who avoided their eyes.

"Okay, what's going on?"

"I told you. I didn't *do* anything." She sat back on the chair.

"Mm-hmm. That's like when you goaded your nephew to—wait, did you have Cook do something with Fergus? Where is he?"

Caroline shrugged. "I honestly don't know."

Laura's brows knit together, her lips tight. "Why does that sound like you're not telling me something? You had better tell me the truth. What if Fergus gets hurt?"

"He won't."

"How do you know that for certain?"

She looked away. "I guess I don't."

Laura sighed deeply. "I'm going downstairs to make the coffee and try and get hold of Cook. And you better come downstairs with a better story than the one you've told thus far." She stomped from the room and down the back stairs.

What had Cook done and why?

Grinding the coffee beans brought an earthy aroma to her nose. She inhaled, enjoying the welcome scent. Laura measured the grounds into the coffeemaker, slamming the reservoir closed with more force than necessary.

Adding water, she punched the button to start the drip process. She pulled mugs from a nearby cabinet, glancing over to the large empty dog bed over by the windows. Voices carried down the stairs as her mother and daughter made their way into the kitchen.

"Now, where were we?" Laura put the milk she'd pulled from the fridge on the table.

The chime for the front door rang.

"What is this? I've just about had it this morning!" She made her way to the front, with her mom and Caroline following behind.

Laura yanked the door open. Hugh again.

"Yes? What do you want?" She blurted out, not caring to disguise her frustration.

"I believe I have something of yours." He went to the car and opened the Range Rover's back door. Fergus bounded out and up the stairs into the house.

Laura turned and gave her daughter a look that said, 'We will talk about this later.'

She bent down and ruffled Fergus's fur. "You had me worried fella."

He licked her cheek causing her to break out in laughter. "Okay, I forgive you, but others have some explaining to do."

Caroline shrugged while Celeste stifled a laugh behind her hand.

Hugh came back up the steps to the door. "I'm sorry. We got off on the wrong foot. I don't—"

"It's fine. Everything's fine. I'll be leaving soon, so thank you again for dinner last night."

"May I ask? Did Georgina put you off?"

Laura's mouth dropped open with surprise. Before she could respond, Celeste came forward.

"I'll have you know that you have a lot of nerve treating my daughter the way you did."

A confused look came over his face. "I beg your pardon?"

Celeste yelled. "You're married!"

His eyes shut as he breathed out a deep groan. "Who shared that with you?"

Laura had regained her voice. "Your wife. Georgina."

"She's not, I mean, she is—"

"What is it? Is she or isn't she your wife?"

"Technically, yes."

"Technically? You Brits have an unusual way of looking at it, but in the US, you're either married or not. There is *no* technically."

His piercing eyes met hers and a smile came to his lips. "I knew you'd have fire in you. I gather this could be our first quarrel."

She fumed, "What are you talking about? Our first? More like our last!"

"Laura, please let me explain." He reached out for her hand, but she pulled it back from him in time. She knew that the electricity she'd felt before would hinder her confidence and anger.

"Please." He waited.

"I don't know. I think we've said everything that needs to be said between us."

Caroline came forward with Fergus on his lead. "You have to take him for his walk, anyway, why not listen to what he has to say?"

Laura took the leash from her before whispering under her breath. "You ought to be ashamed of yourself."

"But I'm not." She winked.

She turned back to where Hugh waited. "I have to walk Fergus. If you want to come along, I guess that's your prerogative."

She took the steps down onto the gravel drive but not before turning back to see her mom and daughter high-five one another. Just wait till she got back. She was going to give them both a talk about staying out of other people's business. Plus, they'd been as outraged about him being married, too. So why the change?

Hugh came over, and they walked down the gravel path in silence. The air was thick with emotion. The pull to reach out to him stronger than anything Laura could ever recall.

They made their way past the tall topiaries, through the evergreens that framed the back garden toward the wooded field. She'd refused to look at him before, but unable to contain herself anymore, she turned to face him.

He took a step forward, placing his hand on her cheek. His eyes met hers.

"Yes?"

Yes.

Chapter Seventeen

Battle Within

"Stop!" She held a shaking hand up between them. Stepping back, she spoke aloud. "What is the matter with you?"

Now facing a wide-eyed Hugh, she glared at him, ever mindful of leaving a sizeable gap between them. The magnetic pull still strong, she couldn't believe she'd almost succumbed.

"You're married! It's obvious by now that I have feelings for you, but no, just no!"

"Laura—" He reached for her hand, but she pulled back and grasped Fergus's leash tighter with both.

"There's nothing to say. You're married. I'm an American and will be leaving soon. We're not just opposites, there's an entire moat of issues for why we can't ever be together. There's no chance for anything beyond the friendship we've shared."

"You're not letting me explain!" He clenched his fists, his eyes blazing with fury.

Laura's brow rose at this new side of him. "Go on."

"All I want you to do is hear me out. Is that too much to ask?"

"I have to think about it. For now, we can't be alone again."

A smile played over his lips. "Why? Don't you trust yourself to behave appropriately with me?"

"Ha ha. Just stop it. I don't appreciate your coy remarks or flirting or whatever it is you're doing."

"How about this? Georgina told me she had invited you to come riding. You can bring your daughter and your mother."

"My mother can't ride on a horse," Laura responded.

"She might like to visit over tea with Dorothea."

"Dorothea? What do you mean?"

"She phoned to let me know they'd be back in a few days."

"Why is Dorothea calling you, of all people?"

"She's my aunt." He pronounced it ah-n-t.

Laura's thoughts swirled. So what that his accent made her weak at the knees? "Wait, did you set up my pet-sitting for them?"

The guilty look on his face gave Laura her answer. "I can't believe you!"

"How else was I to get you to stay longer so that we could spend more time together and so I could—"

"You could what? See if you could get this foolish old American woman into bed!"

"No, well, yes, that had come to my mind. But not in the way you think. I wouldn't be as uncouth as that."

"Then what?"

He stood silent before her. She could see him wrestling with his thoughts.

"Spit it out! What did you want to see?"

"I wanted to see if what I felt for you was infatuation or love."

He stepped closer. "I love you, Laura. I never thought I'd find a love like this. I've never felt this way about anyone in my life. Never. I'm not saying this lightly."

He rubbed his hands through his hair, pacing back and forth. "I can't concentrate. I think of you all the time. I want to be with you. For the rest of our lives."

Laura's mouth flew open before she covered it. "Are you insane? You're married. And I will never be a … what? Your mistress? Something on the side?"

His face darkened in disgust. "You wouldn't. Please. Come on Friday. We'll ride, and you can have others around us. Then I can explain everything. It will give you some time to clear your head and be open to what I want to tell you."

"Why not just tell me now?"

He shook his head. "No, we need to calm down first. I want you to have an open mind when you hear what I have to say."

Footsteps sounding on the gravel caused them to turn to the source. Caroline came around the hedge. "I thought I heard yelling. You okay, Mom?"

"Yes. Thanks."

Hugh spoke to Caroline, "I'm inviting you and your grandmother, and of course your mother, to come riding this Friday. My aunt and uncle, whose home you are staying in, will be back by then. She can keep company with your grandmother. Then we can enjoy a late luncheon if that suits."

"That sounds awesome. Mom? Is that okay with you?"

Laura wanted to turn the invitation down, but she saw the excitement on Caroline's face. She knew that it wasn't just the prospect of going riding, but also seeing Hugh's house, too.

"I suppose that's okay. Just so you know, we've no fancy riding clothes. It'll be jeans and boots or nothing."

He grinned at her. Flushed, she turned away. "I have to walk Fergus. Caroline, why don't you work out the details with Lord Haradon?" She strode off toward the forest path, leaving the pair behind.

So that's why Caroline had acquiesced and cooked up the plot about Fergus. She wanted to see how the other half lived. In some ways, she couldn't blame her. In other ways, she hated that her heart would continue to take a beating.

He loved her. Or so he said. She loved him.

Too bad that wasn't enough.

⁂

The Meriweathers returned from France early. Laura couldn't help wondering if Hugh had a hand in that. Dorothea and Celeste had hit it off like two peas in a pod. Laura had a sneaking suspicion that Dorothea had been sent to work her magic.

Laura dreaded their upcoming meeting, but she couldn't help but remember his words. He had professed his love. It seemed genuine. As much as she wanted to deny it, she knew she had fallen in love with him.

Yet what was the point of pursuing it? She was a middle-class American woman, and he was British aristocracy. The chances of their relationship thriving would have been dismal at best. And then there was Georgina, his gorgeous wife. Why would he even consider leaving her for Laura, a frumpy old lady?

Enough!

She admonished herself. How long and how many years had she spent, never feeling she was good enough, or attractive, or whatever personal shortcomings her mind chose to focus on?

She had lived her life always in the shadow, trying hard to fit in. She never felt right about shining. The other night in the blue gown, she had marveled at the woman who had stared back at her from the mirror. She had noticed the appreciative glances from men and nice compliments from women after Sylvie's help with her style. How could she compete with a woman in her late thirties or forties?

Well, if nothing else, the entire experience had made her confront some harsh truths about herself and what she felt she deserved.

Laura pulled on a new tweed jacket with patches on the elbows. The ladies had all gone into London to shop with Dorothea. Their hostess had taken charge of showing them stores that had been around forever. Laura had purchased the jacket during that trip.

After a morning of shopping, they'd stopped at a pub for lunch for the prerequisite fish and chips. They'd also tried out grilled Halloumi which had been divine. Full of tasty food and the boot, as Dorothea called it, stuffed with bags, the ladies went home to retire to their rooms. While others napped or read, Laura paced back and forth.

What could Hugh say that would make any difference? She should stay behind and let the others go on without her. She could avoid him for the next few days. Then they'd be headed up to London for some sightseeing before flying home.

Home had always filled her with contentment, but this time it felt like returning to a life lived for everyone else. How long had it been since she had lived the life she chose?

A tentative knock on the door stopped her thoughts. She opened the door to find Dorothea.

"May I come in?"

"Certainly. I wanted to thank you again for allowing my mother and daughter to stay here. They have loved being here."

"Of course, my dear. I've enjoyed our talks. Your mother is such fun. I love her stories."

"She's a hoot, all right." Laura waved toward two chairs by a table. "Would you like to sit down?"

"Yes, thank you."

Once settled, the prim and proper woman faced Laura. "I owe you an apology. My part in the subterfuge to get you here is not to be condoned."

"It's okay, though I wondered why you'd need a sitter when you have Cook, plus other staff that come and go."

"I fear that I had an ulterior motive. I'd never heard Hugh with... How shall I put this? It was as if he had discovered life. His voice was filled with laughter and joy, and that's when I realized. My dear, he is in love with you."

Laura wrung her hands. "But he's married."

"Yes, that's true. And today you will find out the reasoning for it. Please, allow this old woman a bit of hope. Hear him out. Don't make up an excuse not to see him today."

Laura sat back, a chuckle escaping her lips. "Are you a mind reader too?"

"No, but I was a young woman once, and I know that you may have considered avoiding the conversation."

She chuckled. "Well, I'll take your 'young woman' as a compliment."

"As a woman in her eighties, you are a young woman. You have a lot more life yet to live and love to give. You just need to be willing to—"

"Let me guess, you were going to say, 'Take a chance.'"

"No, but that is a wonderful phrase. I was going to say that not all is as it seems. So be open to hearing Hugh out." She rose from her seat. "Now, I must find your mother, as we are going to be leaving soon. And you will be joining us?"

Laura nodded. "Yes, I'll come."

"And be open-minded?"

"Okay. I will."

Dorothea came over and hugged Laura, who registered surprise at the gesture. "It's not all stiff upper lip over here, you know." She winked.

Laura laughed. "Good to know. Especially coming from a former Yank. Now let's gather the others."

Chapter Eighteen

Duel Royale

Spying Haradon House, her mother and daughter gave her the side eye with whispered 'wow's.' They exited the vehicles with Dorothea and Celeste already in deep conversation. Laura waited with Caroline as the others went up into the house. A young man drove up in a utility vehicle. "Ay-up. I'm Max. If you come with me, I'll drive you down to the stables. His Lordship will meet you there."

Caroline elbowed Laura good-naturedly. She leaned over and whispered, "His Lordship? Doesn't that sound so perfectly English?"

Laura chuckled, "Try not to be too in awe. They're only regular people. And Hugh puts his pants on one leg at a time, just like every other man."

"How would you know, Mom?" Caroline wiggled her eyebrows.

"Oh, stop it. Don't be silly."

"What fun is that? In fact, I've stopped being silly for far too long." Caroline pouted.

Laura faced her daughter. "You know what—you're right. I'm glad you came over. I think this trip will do you a world of good."

"Come on." Laura hauled herself up onto the seat in the back, with Caroline following. Max tipped his newsboy cap and they set off. Max pulled up in front of a large stone outbuilding. Coupled with some thatched roofs, it felt as if they'd traveled back in time. As they alighted from the vehicle, they waved goodbye to Max, who headed off around the corner.

"There you are." A deep male voice called to them.

Laura turned to see Hugh walking toward them. A groom walked behind him, holding onto the horse's neck ropes.

Caroline turned around so Hugh couldn't see what she said. "Mom, he is a babe. He looks like something you'd see in GQ."

Laura agreed but said nothing. Hugh wore beige riding breeches with well-polished black boots. He sported a dark navy jacket with a crest with an H on his pocket. It must be the Haradon crest. His intense grey eyes met hers, and if she'd been younger, she would have called his gaze swoon-worthy. As it was, her knees wobbled. She wasn't kidding anyone, especially herself, with her act. He was worthy of every single swoon.

He strode up to them. Taking Caroline's hand, he bowed over it. "Nice to see you again. I'm glad that you're able to join us. I've asked my nephew, Trevor, to come along as well."

A young man in his twenties pulled up in his car. Getting out, he called out, "Oy! Just a quick nip in, and I'll join you." He jogged back toward the buildings.

Hugh turned to Laura. "Thank you for coming. I wasn't sure you would."

"I wasn't sure I would either. Dorothea talked me into it."

"Good old auntie. I'll have to share my appreciation with her."

She bristled. "I still made the decision."

He gave a slight nod, "As you should."

After Trevor joined them, they strode over to their horses. Even though Laura wanted to appear self-sufficient, mounting a horse was no small feat. She'd have to accept help. When Hugh placed his hands on her waist to help her up, she couldn't pretend she desired his touch.

After they were all in their saddles, the group set off into the woods. Laura gathered that Hugh had invited the young man to keep Caroline company so they could go off and have their conversation. It wasn't long before they were passed by the younger riders who had set their horses into a run.

"I have to give it to you. You're good at planning." She watched them disappear over the crest of the hill.

"I knew I needed some alone time with you. As we're on horses, I thought you might be more comfortable with the arrangement."

Laura sighed. "I suppose. Now, let's not beat around the bush. What did you want to say to me?"

"Can we stop for a moment?"

She pulled back on the reins to stop the horse from moving. "Okay, you have my full, undivided attention."

Hugh took a deep breath before beginning. "Georgina is my wife. In name only. As you can, or might imagine, I'm a good catch for a woman wanting to marry well."

"And so humble, too."

He laughed. "You have a way of bringing me down a notch."

"Sorry. I concede you've had women throwing themselves at you. Good looks, a title, wealth."

"You think I'm good-looking?"

She blushed. Her heart pounding. "Don't play dumb with me. You're extremely handsome. If we're going to be serious, let's be serious."

"You're right. Georgina came into my life when I was starting my business. An eligible male in his thirties with money and title put a target on my back. My focus was on my career, and I worked long hours. Most days I slept at the office. I never had time for anything but my work. My father was ailing, and he was already talking to me about taking over running Haradon House. Of course, the entire issue of the heir as well. I refused. I wouldn't marry until I found love. The last thing I needed was to fight my way through all these women who wanted me for my money or title. I'd seen too many enter into a farce of a marriage. I refused to do that. Georgina was a student. She'd interned at the firm. We met, and yes, we had a fling. We both realized that was all it was."

Laura huffed, "But you married her."

He held his hands up in a sign of surrender. "Yes, but in name only. To be honest, it was a business deal. I know, I know. I can see by your face this is difficult to accept."

"You could say that."

"We agreed to marry. She would become Lady Haradon and enjoy all the perks that entailed while I enjoyed not having to deal with the constant barrage of women trying to vie for my attention."

"How long has this been?"

"Ten years."

"Ten years!" She threw up her hands, her horse stamping its feet at her outburst.

"I know it sounds horrible. Since we're being honest, I wasn't a saint. I had some dalliances on the side, but it worked for us. No more women flinging themselves at me. No more pressure to marry."

Laura's brow crinkled. "What about an heir and all that? I thought you didn't have children. You could still father one."

"I don't. My sister has a son. I didn't feel it was fair to have a child when I was never home. Now I'm pretty spoiled. While I doted on my nieces and nephews, I had no desire for children at this stage in my life. So my nephew will inherit the estate after I'm gone. After Eton, he came to work for me. He's taken on a leadership role and manages most of the day-to-day operations. Everything was going smoothly. That is until..." He stopped and took Laura's hand. "Until now."

"What's changed?"

"You've changed it. I spoke with Georgina, and she wants to apologize. We hadn't spoken in months, so I hadn't had a chance to speak with her about you. She thought you were another woman after my money. We're both ready to move on. She's been spending time with my friend whom you've met. Anthony."

"Oh, yes. The 'pleasant' anti-American one."

"He's not as bad as all that. He's looked out for me over the years, too. He doesn't hate Americans. He just wanted to get under your craw—is that how you say it?"

"Yes, pretty much. And he succeeded."

"Anyway, he divorced some years back. He knew about my arrangement with Georgina. They have been together ever since. The divorce papers are already in the works. And to ease your mind, they were already in the process before you came into the picture. Meeting you made me more in a hurry to have it finalized. So you wouldn't be any 'home-wrecker,' as you put it."

Laura didn't know what to say. She wanted to believe Hugh, but could she trust him? Had she been enamored with him because he was the first male to pay attention to her since John's death? Or had his house and title put stars in her eyes?

The silence grew between them as he waited for her to respond. "Penny for your thoughts about what I've said?"

She twisted in the saddle. "How old are you?"

He jolted. "I have to admit that wasn't a question I expected. I'm forty-nine. Fifty in June."

Laura's mouth dropped. "Oh, my gosh. You're a decade younger than I am."

"Yes, and according to the data, I'll probably still die before you." He winked.

"Funny. Not."

"Okay, what does it matter if we're not the same age? Or that I'm younger than you?"

"It matters a lot. We're different in so many ways. I'm so different from you. I can see myself doing something stupid to embarrass you. Plus, you still are handsome and will stay that way while I—"

"You are and will always be beautiful to me."

She gulped. He knew how to say the right things.

"Okay, let's get to an even more serious subject. If you think I have money I can bring to help with the upkeep of Haradon House, you're sorely mistaken."

"You never need worry about money with me."

"What are you saying? Are you a... I don't know how to say this without being blunt. Are you a millionaire?"

He hesitated before replying. "Change the m to a b."

"This is too much. How do you know that I'm not just after you for your money?"

"I don't. Even if you are, I don't care. I love you. He took her hand, and turning it over, kissed her palm. "Laura. Dear Laura."

She shivered at the warmth running up her arm. "Hugh, I think this is a big mistake."

"What if it is? Can you say that you don't share feelings for me?"

"I do, but I don't feel confident in them. I need time to think."

"But you're leaving soon."

"Even better. It will give us both some time to be apart and to see what this really is. Plus, for your divorce to go through. Once that happens, you may have a different thought process about this entire thing."

"I won't."

"You don't know that."

"I do." He leaned toward her as the others came back over the hill. Caroline's laughter carried to them, her giddiness with the ride apparent. "Come on, you two old fogies. Mom, you have to see this view."

She clicked her horse and turned back around, with Trevor fast behind her. Hugh gazed at Laura. "What say you?"

Laura grinned, "I'd say you'll be hard-pressed to keep up with me."

"Challenge accepted."

Chapter Nineteen

Emotional Impasse

Worn out from their ride, the four walked their horses back to the stables. As Caroline and Trevor walked into the courtyard, Hugh hopped down from his horse, handing the reins to a stableman. He went over to where Laura sat on her horse, and, placing his hands on her waist, pulled her to the ground.

His hands remained firm against her sides, the heat radiating through her jacket. Laura looked up into

Hugh's eyes. His gaze spoke so much that it almost took the breath from her.

She whispered. "If this will be goodbye, then I suppose there's nothing wrong with a kiss to say it."

Hugh's expression became cloudy. He shook his head. "No. I won't accept goodbye." He leaned toward her and brushed a soft kiss against her forehead. His lips brushed against her hair as they came apart. He pulled back to look deep into her eyes.

"I love you, and I will kiss you when, and only when, there will be no goodbyes between us." Hugh stood back as Max appeared with the utility vehicle. Caroline and Trevor were already at the back, chatting away. Hugh took Laura's hand and helped her into the vehicle before sitting beside her.

Laura's heart pounded at the emotions rushing through her. She didn't know what to think. As the doubts rushed in again, she turned to Hugh.

She did love him. More than anything.

That was why she had to tell him there was no future for them. He needed a younger wife, one who would fit into the society circles he ran in. After marriage, he might change his mind about children. There was no chance of her giving him a child.

Plus, he needed someone who understood British culture, quirks, and long-held traditions. She wouldn't want to give up her American traditions any more than he should have to give up his. It would cost her dearly, but she had to say no to her heart.

For Hugh.

T he remaining days dragged by at a snail's pace. Laura avoided Hugh's calls and Dorothea's pleas to give Hugh a chance.

On the day before they were set to leave, a package arrived for Laura. She found it in her room when she returned from her walk with Fergus.

Tearing at the brown paper, she uncovered a framed document. Done in calligraphy, it was her ancestral tree. Her gaze dropped to the bottom right where her name had been added. To the left of her name there too was John's. Underneath were her children's and grandchildren's names.

Her breath caught when she saw a box to the right. It was blank. Only a space for another name to be added.

The message was clear. There was still a space to be filled. To join her name with another. The gift had tears springing to her eyes. She wiped them away, sucking back in the sobs that fought to escape.

It was for the best. Some loves weren't meant to be.

She leaned down and placed her lips on the blank space. She knew what name should be there. It was written on her heart now and would never be erased.

Chapter Twenty

Coming to Terms

The day for them to leave arrived. After many hugs and goodbyes, the trio took the train back to London.

Playing happy family proved difficult for Laura as she forced herself to focus on seeing the sights with her mother and daughter. Though she tried to force it from her thoughts, Hugh's voice, and her hand in his kept intruding.

Yes, they'd enjoyed the same things, but the old saying must be true that opposites attract.

She also told Dorothea that she appreciated the time spent at her home. Then Laura had side-stepped any conversation about where they'd be staying in London. While she felt comfortable with Dorothea, it would be best not to give her any information she might pass on to Hugh.

She had come to terms with her relationship with Hugh. It had been a wonderful, but brief, affair of the heart. She would treasure their time together forever. For now, it was time to return to the real world.

After arriving and settling in at the luxurious Grosvenor Hotel, the trio enjoyed an outing to the Victoria for a musical.

The following day, they explored the Victoria and Albert Museum. Laura marveled at the beautiful, old architectural elements. It brought to her memory the time with Hugh at Hampton Court, but she forced her mind back to the present.

They were lucky enough to grab a table for lunch in the older part of the museum, and Laura continued to admire the ceiling as they enjoyed their soup and salads.

Later, they wandered through the myriad displays with entire galleries focused on specific items such as ironwork or glass. There was so much to see that Laura berated herself for not having come earlier when she'd been staying in London.

The next day, they'd visit Windsor Castle. This was on her mother's list of places to see. They took the train and made their way into the castle grounds.

After visiting Saint George's chapel inside Windsor Castle, it became apparent Celeste had grown weary.

Leaving the castle, they went across the street to a quaint restaurant. The trio decided on a proper English tea with scones and clotted cream, sandwiches, and some sweets.

The restaurant buzzed with clientele, and all the tables were filled. In one corner, a group of ladies were enjoying a bridal shower.

The young woman, who was being honored, wore a short veil with a tiara that sparkled. Decorated packages and gift bags sat at the table's end, waiting to be opened. Soft laughter came to them as they were escorted to a nearby table.

Caroline caught Laura's eye as they took their seats. She whispered, "Just think, Mom. We could have had a cool bridal shower someplace like this if you'd stop being so stubborn."

"I'm not being stubborn. I'm thinking like a mature adult. Teens follow their hearts. Adults follow their heads. Or should."

Celeste retorted, "If that's the case, then it's not helping you at all. That man is not just a catch. He's a catch and a half. Three-quarters. Um—"

They were interrupted by three tiers of goodies arriving, along with porcelain teapots. Laura waited until they'd helped themselves to tea before continuing.

"I get it. Yes, he's a catch. I agree with you. Just not for me. We're too different." Laura took a salmon sandwich from the tray.

Her mother bristled. "That's what makes the world go round. How boring would it be if everyone were the same! Pshaw. Love is wasted on youth. I'd jump at the opportunity you have with a man who adores you."

Caroline added her thoughts before taking a scone off the porcelain dish. "Oh Mom, don't be so melodramatic. And stop with the woe-is-me false narrative. You don't want to because you're afraid. Pure and simple."

Laura glared at her. She crossed her arms in front of her chest. "I can't believe that you, of all people, are giving me advice while your marriage is falling apart. Have you looked in the mirror?"

Caroline's mouth dropped open. "I can't believe you said that to me."

Celeste clapped her hands. "I can't believe it either. Your mother's just had a breakthrough."

"What do you mean, Gran?"

"I mean, she's finally growing a backbone. She pushed back on what I said earlier. And you need some tough love, and it sounds like she's ready to give it."

Laura gazed at her mother. Then her daughter. "That's true. All this time, I've gone along to get along. I've kept my nose out of your business. Your marriage is failing. And the truth is, it's because you've neglected it." She held up her hand to stop Caroline.

"Let me finish. I'm not saying it's all your fault. Frank's to blame too. There's no such thing as one side to blame. Both sides play a part. There's no fifty-fifty in a marriage. Some days it's ninety-ten. And you're the one taking up the slack. Other days, it's the opposite."

She reached over and took Caroline's hand. "I learned so much about love and marriage when your father was ill. How difficult marriage is. It's easy to give up when it gets tough. It's hard to fight for your marriage when you can't stand the sight of each other. If you can't fight through the 'worst' bits, then you haven't fought for your marriage."

Caroline and Celeste stared at her. Then Caroline broke down in tears. Laura scooted her chair over to her daughter. "You know I love you. I want the absolute best for you. I know that you two love each other. That's why you need to fight for your marriage. And you do that by putting each other first. Over work, over the kids, over anything else that comes between you. You need to have an affair … with your husband."

Caroline wiped her eyes with her napkin. "I've been horrible to Frank. He's been horrible to me, too. But you're right. Something has to give. Maybe when we get home, I'll see if we can take some time away, just the two of us."

"That sounds marvelous. Just don't call me to take care of the kids."

"Mom!"

Laura laughed. "I'm kidding. I love spending time with the kids."

Caroline wrapped her arms around Laura. "I love you, Mom."

"I love you too. More than you know."

"Hey, I want in on that hug action." Celeste quipped.

"Come on." Laura moved between the pair. She bent down to embrace the two women she loved most in the world.

Tears still filled Laura's eyes as she stood. Wiping at them, she was surprised to see an attractive woman from the bridal shower heading toward them.

Oh boy. Here comes trouble. We must have dimmed their fun with all our arguing and tears.

The woman came over to Laura. She spoke in a crisp, proper accent. "I do apologize for overhearing your words—"

Laura got it. Americans tended to be louder than Europeans. Including Brits. "Sorry. A bit of a family thing going on. We'll try to keep it down."

"I think you've misunderstood my intentions. I wanted to say I agree wholeheartedly with your admonitions to your daughter. I couldn't have given better advice to my daughter as she begins her journey in matrimony. Thank you."

The woman held out her hand to Laura. As Laura shook the woman's hand, a strange feeling came over her. Had she finally come into her own as a woman? Why had it taken so long for it to happen? Had she been holding back, not saying what she knew to be true in her heart? Well, no more. "Thank you."

"It would be my pleasure, no, my honor, to pay for your tea service."

"Oh, we couldn't accept that."

Celeste chided her. "Laura, accept the gift."

Laura sighed. "Thank you. That would be wonderful."

The woman called the waitress over and settled it. She would be taking care of the bill. She waved to them as she glided back to the bridal table.

As the trio made their way outside, Caroline said, "How weird was that? I get a telling-off from my mother, but we get our bill paid from it."

"I've always considered those unexpected gifts a bit like angels' kisses," Celeste replied.

"That's a fun way of thinking about it, Gran." Caroline linked arms with her grandmother, helping her off the curb and toward the train station. As they reached the platform, Laura faced them.

"Who's ready to head back to the hotel?"

"Sounds good to me. A night in with a good book sounds great. What do you say, Grandma?"

"You two party-poopers. I'm just getting started. But I'll be okay with staying in tonight."

After all the walking they'd done at the Castle, they were happy to find their seats on the train. Once they arrived back in London, they sprung for a black cab to take them back to the hotel. Laura pointed at the advertisement for Texas on the back of the jump seat. "It's funny. You come here and they're advertising one of our states."

Pulling in front of the hotel, Caroline paid the driver as Laura helped her mother from the car. They had entered the lobby when a woman rising from a chair caught Laura's eye.

It was Georgina.

Chapter Twenty-One

Uninvited Guest

Laura sighed. Dorothea had kept her word of not saying anything to Hugh but most likely her mother had said something to someone. It could have easily gotten back to Georgina. Or the woman had found out some other way.

The woman approached the trio. "Hello, again. Might I have a word?"

Laura sighed. She didn't want to, but she might as well hear her out. "Caroline, will you take mom up to the room? I'll join you shortly."

Laura could see the pair wanted to stay, but she pointed left to the bank of elevators. Celeste stuck out her tongue behind Georgina's back, but Laura refused to engage. They'd drive her crazy about what the conversation entailed later.

Georgina lowered her voice, "Might we take a seat in the lounge?"

Laura nodded. As she followed Georgina into the bar, they sat at a table with comfortable barrel chairs. A server came to take their order, with Georgina ordering a gin and tonic and Laura requesting a merlot.

"First, how did you find me?"

"I have my contacts. Plus, not hard to ask about three American women. And truthfully, your mother let slip what part of town you'd be in. Didn't take much to figure it out from there."

Leave it to Celeste. Whether she did it on purpose or not was another matter. Laura thanked the server, who set the drinks in front of them.

Laura cleared her throat, "Now what can I do for you, Georgina?"

"It's not what you can do for me. It's what I can do for you."

"What would that be?"

"Tell you my marriage to Hugh was one of convenience. It gave me lots of perks, but not in that area if you know what I mean."

"You mean no friends-with-benefits arrangement?"

"Precisely."

"But not always." Laura sipped at her wine.

"No. That is correct. But it was very short-lived. Many years ago. Hugh and I both wanted more, you see."

"More than a title, a major estate, and tons of money?"

"Yes. I know that from the outside, it may sound ludicrous. But it's the truth. Hugh's father was alive and well. So there was no estate or title. Even though Hugh knew that it would come to him at some point, he's always wanted to prove that he is a self-made man. He had an idea and fought for it."

She sipped at her tonic. "Our paths crossed because we worked in the same sectors. We found that we thought alike. We both had ambition. While I wasn't in the same sphere as him, I wanted to be a part of that world. So we made a deal. I would help him, and he would help me."

Laura gazed over at Georgina. "I think if we're going to talk about this, I'm just going to be blunt."

"By all means." Georgina smiled.

"Why get married? You could have become engaged."

"That wouldn't have stopped any woman set out to capture Hugh as her prize. By marrying, I would keep the vultures away from him and he would help me gain entry to places I never could on my own. Doors opened because I was Hugh's wife."

"Yes, but that was years ago. A decade! If it was only for convenience, why keep it up?"

"He wasn't seeing anyone, and I enjoyed playing the part of Lady Haradon. Over the years, we left it as neither of us were looking elsewhere. We live separate lives, occasionally coming together for certain events. Like the dinner the other night. I could see your feelings for him right away."

Laura blushed. "What? I didn't—"

Georgina's laughter stopped any further remarks. "You do. That's why I said what I did in the ladies' room. I went into attack mode. Hugh hadn't explained your relationship."

"And now? Hugh said that you two have divorce proceedings in process."

"I believe that you've met Hugh's friend, Sir Anthony."

Laura pulled a face.

Georgina smiled. "I'll take that as a yes. He isn't like that. As Hugh's friend, and as his 'wife,' we protect him from, well, shall we say, gold diggers."

"Like me?"

"No offense."

"Some taken."

Georgina's eyebrow shot up. "I can see why Hugh likes you. You're not afraid to speak your mind. Now I didn't know anything about you. I didn't know that Hugh had gone head over heels. As I said, I tried to put you off. He was so cross when I told him later about our encounter."

"Well, you succeeded."

"Look, I've come to plead his case. We are already in the divorce process, so I can marry Anthony. Hugh adores you. I've never seen him like this before. He can't stop talking about you. It's a bit tiring, to be honest. I knew him before we decided on our subterfuge. Hugh has been a dear friend for years. But that's all. I believe he has been waiting for you his entire life. Please reconsider." She took a swig of the drink, setting it down on the round table. Pulling some pounds from her clutch, she laid them on the table. "I hope that we will meet again under better circumstances, Laura. Don't delay." She strode off, leaving Laura staring into her wine goblet.

So now Hugh was sending Georgina? What next? She glanced at the time. Tomorrow they would leave for home. She could have this memory of a fleeting affair to remember when the days drew long. She picked up her purse, before tipping the goblet back, to finish her drink.

Now to face the gauntlet of her mother and daughter.

Chapter Twenty-Two

Turning the Page

"Grandma!" the kids called to her as Laura entered their house.

"Hello, you two. What's going on in your world?"

They bubbled over with excitement as they shared their current events, and affairs of the teenage heart, and asked about her trip.

They'd already set up a board game and crusty dough from pizza met her nose.

Caroline and Frank had gone off for the weekend, leaving Laura to stay with the kids.

After returning home, her mom had given up on changing Laura's mind about Hugh.

Celeste had then headed to Florida to spend the colder months.

And while things hadn't returned to the old normal, she felt comfortable again.

Though even with adding in lots of activities, she struggled to get Hugh off her mind.

It would take time, but she knew that just like her life after John, each day would bring her closer to her old way of life.

Arriving home the following day, she plopped her purse down on the kitchen counter. The doorbell rang.

Pulling it open, a stocky man from a delivery company stood holding a large cardboard envelope. "Sign here, please."

He held out a small device for Laura to sign. "Have a great day." He sprinted down the sidewalk to his waiting van.

Laura gazed down at the envelope. It was addressed to her with a return address she didn't recognize in England.

She pulled the tear strip from the large envelope. Inside was another envelope, wrapped in tissue paper.

Setting down the large packaging, she unfolded the paper to reveal a large four-by-six envelope.

Her name was printed in beautiful calligraphy and the back had a seal on it.

Taking up her reading glasses, she made her way over to the chair in the living room. She opened the envelope.

Inside was a wedding invitation for Georgina and Sir Anthony Wadsworth. The date was for the following May.

So Georgina and Hugh's divorce had gone through.

She couldn't help feeling saddened for Hugh. Even though they hadn't been a true married couple, from what Georgina had said, they'd been good friends. Would this change that?

A slip of paper fell at her feet. She must have missed it. It was a brief note from Georgina.

Please come and celebrate the future. G

Celebrate the future. She laid the invitation in her lap.

She couldn't go back. It would open the wound in her heart again.

◆━◦◉◦━◆

The following weeks brought cooler weather and time for book club again.

Laura was looking forward to catching up with the ladies in person. She was happy to discuss the new book. She was done with the ghosts of past wives.

Donning a new dress with a pair of heeled brown boots, she made her way to the restaurant where they'd first met.

In a tote bag, she'd brought an assortment of gifts for the ladies, all from Harrod's or Selfridge's.

Upon entering the restaurant, Betsy waved at her. "We're over here!" Laura waved back before heading in their direction.

Sylvie spoke first. "You look terrific. I love your new look."

Laura fawned and patted her hair. "It's down to my stylist. You should try her." She winked.

"Speaking of—look!" Sylvie pulled out a card. *Styling with Sylvie. Uniquely you. Uniquely beautiful.*

"Oh, that's wonderful." She wanted to ask more but decided to leave that discussion about Sylvie's life changes for another time.

Laura hung her jacket on a nearby coat rack before taking her seat. "You ladies all look great. You'll have to catch me up with what's been going on."

Claire rubbed her cheek.

"Are you okay, Claire?"

"Yes, but having some dental issues. I'm considering going to Mexico to have the work done."

"I don't know if I'd want to have any surgery or dental work done there," Shirley responded.

"They're trained just like everyone else here in the States. You're just paying their pricing. It's a win-win," Betsy replied.

Laura laughed. "Betsy, I think I'm going to start thinking of you as the connector. What have you got going on?"

"I'll be heading to San Antonio soon for a pet sit."

"So no trips abroad?" Francis asked.

"Not right now." Betsy grabbed a piece of bread from the basket the server left.

"So sounds like Claire and Betsy are traveling soon, Sylvie has a new business, what about you two?"

Shirley shrugged. "Still looking for a renter."

Laura knew that took a lot for Shirley to admit. She'd been so closed off before about what was going on in her life.

"Oh, what can we do to help?"

"Angela contacted me to let me know she knew someone who needed a place. So we'll be meeting soon."

"Where is Angela? She started this group and yet we never see her," Francis asked.

Claire said. "It is weird. She'll text about things. She told me she had something come up and that's why she couldn't make it today."

Laura spoke to Francis. "What about you? Anything fun in your life?"

"I'm thinking about taking some dance lessons. I've always loved to dance, so why not?"

"That does sound fun. If I didn't have two left feet that is," Betsy replied.

Shirley interjected, "Laura, tell us about your trip. What did you love most?"

Laura swallowed. What she had loved most was Hugh. She took a sip of water as the expectant faces waited for her answer.

"Well, I can tell you, it wasn't some of the food!" Laughter broke the tension.

"Of, course, I'm sure people that visit here from other countries think the same thing about our food. Of course, you can't beat their tea, scones, and clotted cream."

Laura described the places she'd stayed, the people she'd met, and the various sites she'd seen.

She shared some pictures of her in front of the homes as the ladies oohed and aahed.

"You look like the lady of the manor," Betsy said. "Who's the woman standing beside you?"

"That is the lady of the manor. Dorothea. She and my mom had a fun time together."

Francis interjected. "Tell us what we really want to know. How did you leave it with Hugh?"

Laura deflected talk of Hugh by sharing about their wonderful friendship, but she wasn't sure she fooled any of them.

She also didn't share about the recent invite to Georgina's wedding next spring.

After a delightful evening, the ladies said goodbye until their next meeting.

That evening, Laura found she couldn't sleep. Something that Betsy had said during their meal had wormed its way into her mind.

In her haste to do what she believed was the right thing, had she lost the chance to do the best thing?

Did I make the biggest mistake of my life?

It went round and round in her mind until she fell asleep.

Laura slept late the following morning.

Rising from her bed, she heard the chirp on her phone. It was a group chat. They were wishing Claire a safe journey as she was headed to Mexico.

Betsy wrote, 'Don't forget to take a chance!'

Francis typed in her reply, "That was for Laura. We need a new one for Claire."

"Okay, like what?" Shirley asked.

"Hmm, how about something to do with words? Since Claire used to be an English professor."

"How about 'Write your own ending'?"

Claire responded, "I'm not dead yet."

"Okay, how about 'Enjoy a plot twist'?"

"As long as the plot twist doesn't include all of my teeth falling out with the dental procedure, then sure."

Smiling emojis followed.

Laura was about to set her phone down when another chime came through.

It read, 'Just because you're home doesn't mean yours ends. Take a chance!'

More emojis followed.

'Got it.' She set the phone down.

After showering and dressing, she had pulled items from the fridge to make avocado toast when the doorbell rang. She set the bread on a plate.

Did I order something I forgot about?

She pushed her hair off her face and opened the door.

Hugh.

Her heart leaped.

Flustered at his unexpected arrival, Laura fought for the right words.

He showed her his hands, holding the hat she'd seen him wear on their first meeting. "As you can see, I've come with my hat in my hands. I only ask that you hear me out."

"Come in," she managed to squeak out.

Shutting the door behind them, he sat his hat down on the hall table.

The air was thick with emotion as neither spoke nor moved. He took her in his arms and pulled her to him.

This time Laura would give no excuses, no reasons as to why their union couldn't work. He had come all the way from England to speak to her.

She loved him.

She wanted him.

And she would not deny herself any longer.

When his soft warm lips met hers, the world dissolved.

In that moment and time, they were the only two beings on the planet.

Far beyond mere passion, the kiss had developed into the joining of two soulmates.

When they came up for air, he kissed her cheeks, her hands, and her forehead before wiping happy tears from her eyes.

She gazed into his eyes. "You came."

"I did."

"I love you." The words spilled from her lips.

He gathered her hands together, kissing them. "I love and adore you. I wanted to ask you out and do this properly, but I can't wait. I have to know now."

He went down on one knee, opening a black velvet box containing a stunning ring.

"Laura, my darling, will you marry me?"

Doubts and fears rose their ugly heads. This time, she fought back against them.

She struggled to breathe.

"What say you?"

Life had given her a second chance, and she refused to say no any longer.

"I say absolutely, positively, yes."

He rose from his kneeling position.

They laughed as he placed the ring on her shaky finger. Taking her back into his arms, she put her arms around his neck.

Her entire being buzzed with excitement.

Their lips met. The world faded. The kiss was sweet with the love that would carry them through all of their days.

Shaking, she drew back, "What about—"

He put his finger on her lips before stroking her hair.

"We have all the time in the world to figure everything else out. As long as we're together, we have everything we need. Are you ready to take a chance on us?"

She burst out laughing.

"What?"

"It's something some good friends said to me. I'll tell you one day."

She gazed into his eyes.

"For now, kiss me again."

Thank you for reading Charming Chapter.

If you enjoyed Laura's story, then you'll enjoy more of the Boomer Babes Book Club Romances.

To stay on top of upcoming releases, and giveaway opportunities along with other similar author romances, then sign up for my newsletter at my website or look me up and follow me on social media.

Additionally, I used the Five Love Languages to help me determine what each character desires. Can you guess what I chose for Laura's?

Want to read the next Boomer Babes Book Club Romances?

Here's a glimpse into Claire's story.

Surprising Chapter

Book Two

After a successful academic career, Claire's ready to retire. With her book club encouraging her to try new things, she heads to Mexico. She intends to have dental work done before indulging in relaxation and reading.

Meeting her attractive host, Pat Norby, he turns out to be a fellow book enthusiast.

On a night out, Claire questions her feelings for Pat after he heroically saves her from a nasty fall.

What will happen to Claire's new chapter on love when the hidden truth is revealed?

Finally, while I'm a semi-literate and educated human who wrote this book, any mistakes you may find are all mine.

May you find your own Happy-ever-after!

Lori